THE SPIDER:
MASTER OF THE DEATH-MADNESS

## MASTER OF MEN!

# MASTER OF THE DEATH-MADNESS

*By Grant Stockbridge*

STEEGER BOOKS • 2020

# CHAPTER 1
## PRIESTESS OF DEATH

A CLAMMY fungus of a moon had fastened itself upon the horizon and swelled there, feeding. Its light played across the boat-deck of the *Plutonic* with a heavy, sweet whiteness. The couples that strolled there moved slowly, voices muted. Wentworth felt a sharp, anxious restlessness as he planted himself grimly by the rail, nailing his feet to the deck to still the clamor of his mind.

Nita van Sloan, her slim, round arms leaning on the rail, watched him anxiously. "What is it, Dick?" she asked softly. "Ever since last night, when you saw that Egyptian…."

"Damn the Egyptian!" Wentworth made his voice deliberately harsh. "Damn the Egyptian. It's not that, but there's something—something evil—hovering over this boat."

"But it began last night!"

"Yes." Wentworth spoke the words slowly through stiff lips. "It began last night!"

They stood there by the rail with the pale, moon-coated sea murmuring past the steel sides of the liner. About them, lovers murmured in the shadows; from the promenade deck below, the strains of a Viennese waltz by Richard Strauss strummed out into the moon-laden night.

There was soft laughter and the wash of the swelling sea. Evil seemed far away, yet Nita did not scoff at the fears shown in

1

Anubis brought a wild suicide mania to America!

every line of Wentworth's erect stiff braced body. For secretly, he was more than the wealthy sportsman and dilettante of the arts that he seemed. His other life was furtive and death-ridden, a hidden, stealthy thing of the nights—and the Underworld. He was a lone wolf of justice and champion of oppressed humanity, its shield and buckler against the criminal jackals that preyed upon it. He was the Spider!

And the Spider did not speak lightly of evil. He was too gentle, too tender a lover, to blot the glamorous night with useless vaporings. He was too courageous to take fright from vague nothings. But through years of ceaseless struggle and hourly danger—not alone from the Underworld but also from the police who considered his brand-marked executions of criminals only murder—he had developed an uncanny feeling like the sixth sense of bats. Flying in the dark, scarcely seeing, the convoluted facial feelers of a bat received, apparently, an impact of air waves which forewarned the animal of obstacles in its path. So something—thought waves?—warned the Spider of danger.

"If only I could discover some reason for all this," Wentworth muttered. "I might...."

Nita's white hand touched the sleeve of his drill dress jacket and he ceased speaking, turned toward her in the shadows, eyes questioning. She shook her head and dimly he heard the approaching mutter of voices—a man's, excited, sharp expostulations; a woman's soft, slurred, somehow... mocking!

Nita whispered. "It's that Egyptian woman!"

WENTWORTH'S FOREARM hardened beneath Nita's hand; he drew her close, an arm tenderly about her shoulders.

His mind was blazing with thoughts that ran like quick, liquid flame. It had started last night, this restlessness that presaged to him one of those visitations of hell upon earth which great criminals periodically brought. It began last night when the entertainment committee had decided upon an amateur night. Wentworth had improvised upon his priceless Stradivarius—which was never far from him—and his fingers rebelliously had tripped out harsh and disturbing music from the violin, soul-embittered stuff that laid a hush upon his audience—a silence as different from the customary, polite attention as death is different from sleep. In the quiet that had gripped the passengers after his last, almost dissonant chord, his eyes had strayed, toward Nita as always, and had met—those of the Egyptienne!

For a full, long second—as long as the waiting silence of the audience—their eyes had held and the dark, velvet-soft gaze of the woman had hardened with points like steel and then had glowed with an internal flame that was lambent and lovely and, somehow, starkly cruel. Then a burst of applause, simultaneous, overwhelming as nearby thunder, crashed out. Men stood and clapped their hands; women's handkerchiefs and fans waved high in the air. Wentworth bowed somberly, feeling still the impact of the woman's gaze, and refusing an encore, returned to Nita's side.

"That woman, the Egyptienne, Nephtasu, tried to hypnotize me," he said harshly, "and damned near succeeded!"

The Egyptienne's uncle, Jamid Bey, had been called on by the committee to display the powers of hypnotism he had discussed at the captain's table several nights before. He had been graceful about refusal, but quite firm. Now, however, he rose from the audience, tall, built with the strongness and the prideful carriage of a lion, and turned his dark hawk's face toward Wentworth.

"Thank you, sir," he had said with that resonant, quiet voice of his, black hair like a crown on his head, "for a very genuine moment of emotion. May I ask the name of the thing you played? It is very like—like something out of the past of my country."

Wentworth had arisen and bowed quietly, with the dignity that clothed him always. "You have a good ear," he returned gravely. "It is a little improvisation of my own, quite impromptu, upon a temple chant out of Egypt. It has... echoes." His eyes grew shrewd then. He had been curious about this man, conscious of his magnetic power and his potentialities, whether for evil or good it was hard to say. "Won't you give us a demonstration, sir, of your undoubtedly remarkable hypnotic powers? I, for one, am very anxious, and..." The wave of his hand brought a splatter of applause that swelled and grew.

Jamid Bey perceptibly hesitated, then shrugged and made his way slowly to the platform. His departure had revealed his ward, as she styled herself, in the next seat, and Wentworth's puzzled, quick eyes swept her. She was superbly dressed in what would have made another woman only conspicuous—a gown of sequins which, rising high in a point in front, looped about her exquisite throat and left the rounded symmetry of her shoulders and back completely bare. The gown was dark, sea-green, and the towering dark flame of her hair and the golden quality of her skin, it clothed her in splendor. As he glanced at her, the woman's head turned slowly and her mouth, too long and slim for absolute beauty, had moved lazily in an enigmatic smile. Her eyes, Wentworth saw, were not black as he had thought, but green.

Jamid Bey's demonstration was ordinary, disappointing. Wentworth caught throughout it a sense of mockery in the man, convincing proof that he was deliberately minimizing his ability. And with wonder as to why he should do such a thing had come that sense of impending evil Wentworth had felt too often to ignore—*the warning of the Spider!*

THESE THOUGHTS flicked through his mind as he stood by the rail in the moonlight, simulating with Nita the tender tryst of lovers while the mutter of the approaching voices, whose temper was already clear, became distinct words.

"… but I love you, 'Tasu!" the man cried. "You gave me hope. You can't deny that…?"

The woman's voice was almost lazy, quietly amused, the accent subtle, an indefinable slurring of words that gave her an aura, like the scent of temple jasmine, of the East. "I do deny it!"

"But your eyes, 'Tasu! Your eyes gave me hope! I swear it…!"

Wentworth moved his head impatiently and Nita breathed words against his face. "She has encouraged him, no question of that. It's that youngster with the quaint eyes…"

Wentworth's arm on her shoulders silenced her.

"… a very ridiculous boy," Nephtasu declared slowly. "You

were amusing for a while, but now you bore me. Leave at once." There was no change in her voice, but somehow it had become cold.

"I'll kill myself!" The man screamed the words, screamed them with a broken, hysterical shrillness that caused a hush over the boat-deck, froze the strolling couples, rang flatly out over the gilded sea. "I'll kill myself unless...."

Nephtasu's voice was filled with a sudden force of hatred like the flick of a whip. "By all means kill yourself, fool! There is no hope—but there is the sea!"

Wentworth sprang from Nita's side. "Don't, you fool!" he cried.

But the man moved too swiftly for him. Wentworth had seen his first move, an awkward hand-vault over the low railing, and now the man poised beside a davit of the life-boat, hands thrown up wildly, white face lifted to the white, dead face of the moon. Before Wentworth could even reach the rail, he plunged, silently, swiftly. There was a small, sullen splash and the sound died swiftly.

"Man overboard! Man overboard!" Wentworth's shout rang out and then a dozen frightened voices picked it up, screaming, shouting that dread warning.

Wentworth tore at his coat, whirling with the swift precision of perfectly coördinated muscles and body. He had a single fleeting glimpse of the Egyptienne. The vision stayed with him as he raced aft along the boat-deck, crying for Nita to throw a lighted life-ring overboard. Nephtasu had stood motionless, chin lifted imperiously, the glory of her hair snaring the vagrant moonbeams and Wentworth had a memory of the stark cruelty that was in the flame of her eyes. It was there now, mocking him and his efforts to save the boy she had ordered so imperiously to death.

Wentworth raced sternward until he had reached the utmost limit of the deck. He kicked off his pumps, and sprang to the rail. For an instant he poised there, a clean-limbed, stalwart figure against the moonlit sky. Then his body arched outward in a javelin-smooth dive. He had two thoughts beside the necessity of the man's rescue: The cold cruelty of Tasu and the certainty that this was but a forewarning of the evil to come!

The water was a tepid, violent smack; then, as he struck deeper with the impetus of a sixty-foot dive, it turned cold and bitter. He was up instantly, glimpsing the two fiery flares of the life-preserver Nita had tossed overboard. Then he was lining out for the spot where the man bobbed in the wake of the great liner. He apparently was making no effort to swim, but now and then his arms flashed....

SO MUCH Wentworth saw as he caught a deep breath. Then his arms began to swing in a swift, perfect precision of a racing crawl; his kicking feet made a small, white froth that widened into a wake behind him as he sped along the tepid surface. Despite his really remarkable speed, he was still twenty feet away when he saw the man go down, flinging his arms upward in a last wild gesture that might have been an appeal to the heavens, or a last worshipful salaam to the woman who had doomed him.

Wentworth's stroke was already at its formidable maximum and he did not change it. But as he reached the spot where the man had sunk, he sucked in repeated, deep breaths, and seconds after the victim had disappeared, he nosed under and shot downward, stroking strongly. Useless to attempt to see, and if this one dive failed, useless to try again. There was only one thing in his advantage. A swimmer could drive his body down more swiftly than an unconscious man would sink.

About twelve feet down, Wentworth lungs began to ache for air; the drumming of pressure sounded in his ears. His strenuous dash had set his blood to pumping swiftly and his oxygen-starved body cried out for air. Wentworth forced some of the spent breath from his lungs, surged more strongly toward the depths.

His sweeping arms circled fiercely once, again—ah! What was that? His swift finger-tips brushed something. He drove downward another stroke—and grasped clothing!

In that last furious effort, Wentworth exhausted his strength, drove the last cubic inch of usable air from his lungs, destroyed his body buoyancy. And now he must fight his way to the surface, his clothing a sodden anchor, the unconscious form of a man a drowning weight, his efficiency handicapped by the loss of the arm that supported the man. The drumming in his ears was a thunderous assault on his senses now; the ache of his lungs was unbearable. He must—*must* breathe! Yet breath now would mean strangulation, suffocation in the salty dregs of the sea. His will fought against the subconscious command of his brain and his will was battered by the black, cold death of the water; by the leaden fatigue of every oxygen-starved muscle.

Upward, upward he fought, legs and one arm stroking frantically. His will still commanded stubbornly and his laggard body obeyed. Upward! His eyes strained against the blackness. Dear God! Was that a glimmer of silvery light there above him? Was it? Stroke and kick. Stroke and kick! Upward, and—head and shoulders burst through the surface; a great draught of life-giving air gusted into his throat and lungs and the drumming ache diminished while his body drank in the blessed oxygen. He was panting, weak from struggle, but he still had the will to roll over upon his back, and cradling the unconscious man's chin in his elbow, propel himself along feebly. Swiftly then, his exuberant strength recuperated, and finally he was able to look around, to see where the *Plutonic* lay....

He trod water, breathing easily now, noticed that the life-ring blazed on the surface a little over a hundred yards away. The *Plutonic* was swinging about in a great arc almost a half-mile distant, preparing to lower a boat, a great floating city of twinkling lights. Slowly, swimming on his side, Wentworth propelled himself and his unconscious burden toward the life ring. His sharp exhaustion had left him, but it had been replaced by a leaden weariness, a vast oppressive weight. But this was a thing he could combat, too, with will. Soon he would be within the white circle of the life-ring's light, and then....

SOMETHING STRUCK the water six inches to the left of Wentworth's head. It was not a loud splash nor the flat washing slap of something falling. It was a throaty *thuck* and was followed by a high, thin wailing, *screee!* A single, harsh curse squeezed out between Wentworth's lips. Someone was shooting at him with a light-powered rifle!

No one on board would
have any inkling as to the
cause of their death....

Good shooting, that, coming within six inches of a man's
head, not too clearly seen in the blaze of the ring's lights—
at a range of better than six-hundred yards and on the first

shot! Such good shooting that it might well be better. The next bullet....

It whipped by over Wentworth's head with a sound like a needle jabbed through a taut drum-head. Yards behind him,

it threw a narrow jet of white water into the air. No sound of the first shot had reached Wentworth. Obviously, it was from a silenced rifle. There would be no chance of detection aboard the ship and the rifleman was getting the range…!

This new peril helped drive the fatigue from Wentworth's body. He set grimly to saving himself and his unconscious charge. He knew now, knew with terrible certainty, that his forebodings were justified, that some man-actuated horror was waxing to filthy bloom there upon the ship. He must return there, ferret out this menace before it struck….

It would be simple to save himself from that sniping rifle if he were alone and free to swim rapidly about—easy to dodge at range of better than six hundred yards. But with this burden—

Still he could not abandon the man to his fate—and there were yet strategies to try… Wentworth clamped a hand over the man's nostrils and mouth, and by a strenuous effort, drove their two bodies beneath the surface. Scarcely had he done that when the third bullet struck, making a deafening sound, so close that if he had not dodged, that bullet would have drilled his head!

No one on board the ship would have had any inkling as to the cause of their death. It would be simply that an heroic attempt to save a fellow passenger had failed!

He was battling now to keep beneath the surface, struggling back toward the curtain of darkness behind the light. It was no more than fifty feet, but he could not go straight toward it, lest the rifleman… Bursting lungs forced him to the surface and, heartbeats later, lead cracked past his head. He dived again.

Thoughts flitted with remarkable clarity through his fatigue-weighted mind. There seamed no question now that Nephtasu had deliberately goaded the man—perhaps hypnotized him—into that leap overboard. It might be that the uncle was shooting at him now to prevent a revelation of the fact. But why, *why?*

Again and again Wentworth submerged and finally he reached his goal—the darkness directly behind the life-ring. Its two magnesium flares made out the lifeboat which had been lowered and was oaring its way swiftly toward the light, but he estimated that he must somehow keep afloat at least ten minutes more and also support the dead weight of the unconscious man. He shut his teeth grimly. Since the bullets no longer threatened....

The shooting became frenzied. The rifleman was pumping out a fan of bullets, pricking the water at intervals a foot apart directly through the life-ring's glare. The lead followed an almost perfect arc; then lifted and began a second quarter-circle a couple of feet beyond the first. It was incredibly perfect shooting. Wentworth suspected the man had rigged a brace and was aiming mechanically. With a rising sense of despair, he realized that the third arc of bullets would find them both unless he could make some new desperate effort.

The gunman's attack changed suddenly; the bullets cracked in a slightly increased elevation each time so that the assassin sewed a seam of narrow water jets in a straight line from the life-ring toward the darkness, ploughing the last three only a yard from where Wentworth floundered. Desperately, scarcely able to wallow into motion, Wentworth worked himself and his charge directly toward the ripples where the bullets had struck. The rifleman would not shoot twice at the same spot... He was almost upon it when vicious lead fanned his face and he flung frantically backward, fought away while the water that he had thought a sure refuge was churned to fury by narrowly spaced bullets. Another minute and Wentworth would have been trapped by the rifleman's cleverness. The man had deliberately built up a pattern of fire to give the idea that he would not shoot again at the same place, allowed time for Wentworth to reach the spot where last his bullets had struck, then riddled that spot again.

But it was the assassin's last effort. Three minutes after the final storm of lead, the rescue boat drifted up to the life-ring and, hearing Wentworth's weak hail, hauled the two exhausted men over the gunwale. Blankets were thrown over them and strong, biting whisky burned Wentworth's throat. He continued to lie on the bottom of the boat even though revived. It was barely possible that the assassin might think it worth while to kill him and his companion, even in the life boat, or when they mounted the ladder to the deck.

## CHAPTER 2
## SUICIDE MANIA

PROLONGED CHEERING sounded long before the lifeboat came alongside the *Plutonic* and was lifted upward on creaking davits. Not until then did Wentworth, still weary but entirely recovered otherwise, sit upright and spring to the deck. The man he had saved was lifted on a stretcher and hurried away toward the sick bay. A slim, young girl in fluffy evening-dress, her face stained with tears, ran along beside the unconscious man, crying through a handkerchief she wedged against her mouth. The Egyptienne, Nephtasu, was nowhere in sight....

Scarcely had Wentworth set foot on deck when a turbaned Hindu in immaculate, white house-garb, his faithful body servant, Ram Singh, stepped forward and held a rich-hued flannel dressing robe for him. Wentworth thrust his arms into it gratefully, for the wind was blowing colder and a black cloud was stalking the moon. Ram Singh then knelt, fitted slippers to his master's feet. His dark face was as utterly impassive as if it were an hourly event for his master to leap overboard. But there was glittering pride in his eyes, an almost dog-like devotion when he received Wentworth's thanks with a salaam, a lifting of cupped hands to his forehead. He vanished then, slippers patting the floor softly, and the crowd thronged forward to congratulate Wentworth. Among the first was the Egyptian man, Jamid Bey, his grave, strong face admiring.

"A brave thing to do, sir," he declared, offering a small, slim-fingered hand. "Undoubtedly the boy would now be dead but for your prompt action."

Wentworth smiled, bowing, but his eyes were hard and intent. Was he mistaken or had there been a veiled threat in those words—but for *you*, he would be dead—a promise to pay back a disservice? Wentworth's expression did not betray his thoughts, though his was no stiff, expressionless poker face. He protected himself from the eyes of the curious and those of his enemies by a mobility of expression that obeyed his slightest will. Even his eyes revealed nothing.

"I shall do myself the honor of calling you later in the evening, sir," Wentworth said. "There is a matter I should like to discuss with you."

"By all means," Jamid Bey replied. His accent was less subtle than his words, but the voice, while resonant, had a certain harshness that held arrogance, almost contempt. His eyes, meeting Wentworth's as he turned away, were inscrutable.

Suddenly, without warning, a shot rang out!

Wentworth saw Jamid Bey dodge aside. His own muscles made him to spring warily aside, although the direction of the shot—it's slightly muffled sound—did not indicate an attack. Wentworth's eyes narrowed on the Egyptian's back. He recognized, however, the quick movements of a man trained in the hard school of deadly battle. Then, somewhere among the crowd, a woman screamed and there was a half-panicky stir. Nita stepped to Wentworth's side, hand on his arm. A ship's officer shouted clearly.

"Nothing to be afraid of, ladies," he called. "An accidental shot. Probably...."

BUT WHEN they located the source of that shot, it did not appear accidental. An aged architect had messily blown off the top of his head by putting the muzzle of a thirty-eight caliber revolver in his mouth. And the search revealed a second suicide.

A young girl had hanged herself with a silken scarf whose loose end, streaming in graceful folds from her throat, seemed too gay for a hangman's rope. Gazing at her distorted face—he had joined the search after a swift change of clothing—Wentworth felt horror grow within him....

In a space of minutes, his face became haggard and harsh with bitter lines. It was strange, very strange, that these people had killed themselves—as strange as those silenced rifle shots that had tried to keep him from the rescue of a third person who sought to join the stark company of the dead. It was strange, too, that for hours beforehand he had felt the cold touch of impending tragedy. Another shot in a distant corridor jerked at his muscles, but he did not follow the others toward the scene. He knew already what they would find; he was sure. The grinning specter of suicide had boarded the ship to stay.

A rough curse twisted Wentworth's mouth. It seemed certain that there was work here for a defender of humanity—for the Spider!

It was conceivable that the man who had leaped overboard might have done so in the momentarily intense agony of Nephtasu's scorn. But these others, what could be the motive for their self-destruction? This venerable, gray-haired Briton who had blown out his brain, and this lovely creature whose face was distorted into a travesty on life?

Wentworth turned, frowning, from the room of death and, in the corridor, lighted one of his privately blended cigarettes with deliberate, steady hands. He had discarded formal dress for dark tweeds that were habitual with him and he was a somber, brooding figure there in the half-light, a man with square but not heavy shoulders, carried with the self-confidence of the physically and mentally able; a strong, lean profile, shown in the back-glow of his lighter, with an intelligent nose beneath a cap of crisp, black hair. The gray-blue eyes, half hidden now beneath thoughtful lids, could be rapier-sharp and piercing as a thrust. There was always a touch of arrogance in the poise of his shapely head, though his face turned boyish with a smile and the tip-tilted brows carried a subtle hint of mockery. There was none of that now in his somber mien.

He turned firmly down the hall, promising himself grimly that he would have a conference this night with Jamid Bey. His right hand rose almost subconsciously, touched the spot beneath his left arm where, masked by well-padded clothing, one of his twin forty-five automatics lay snug in a clip holster. He was within three yards of a companion-way that led to A deck, where Bey had a suite and private deck, when a girl burst from the darkened entrance, screaming.

Her shriek soared intolerably, rising as she stood with stiff arms outthrust before her. Dark curls wore about her head and her ivory, satin dress caressed the rounded contours of shoulders and breast. But all this was marred now. Beneath the tulle that fluttered from her throat there was a horrid growing redness and one of her out-stretched hands held a razor that was red, too. For a long moment, she stood there screaming away her life. Then she toppled, face down, with a crash like falling trees. Her fists bounced limply, her feet drummed a little....

But Wentworth, a bitter breath caught between his teeth, did not wait for the hue and cry to follow. In the darkness of the steep companionway, he had glimpsed a tall, white figure that moved fleetingly. In two long strides, he leaped over the girl's pitiful body, reached the steps. The figure was nearly at the deck above and Wentworth's gun flashed to his hand with the swiftness of a sword leaving its scabbard.

"Halt!" he cried sharply. "Halt or—!"

THERE WAS no hesitation in the fleeing figure, nor in Wentworth's action. He did not level his weapon, poised there at his hip; he merely squeezed the trigger. Mingled with the crashing gun-thunder that hammered in his ear-drums came an inarticulate cry, a thump of a colliding body. Then the white figure vanished. Wentworth raced upward. He could not have missed. His familiar guns were mere extension of his body, projections of nerve-ends into space. His aim was as sure as a thrown beam of light. But the fugitive sped on....

Seconds later, Wentworth burst out onto A deck, poised a moment with his gun-muzzle sweeping. He caught a fleeting glimpse of the white figure again, but it was plunging toward the sea. A subdued splash and Wentworth sprang to the rail. The yellow lights of the boat slid unperturbed over the fading ripples—that was all....

Had someone killed the girl, then leaped overboard? No reason, no sense in that. It was mad, utterly mad. Wentworth whirled about, his narrowed eyes probing the shadows, seeking some sign of the person in white who could not, simply could not, have leaped overboard—but there was nothing at all except the screams and shouts as others found that pitiful body in the corridor and raced to discover the source of that blasting shot.

Men and women were darting along the deck now, flitting objects in the shielded glow of lights. There was no moon now, nothing but dark hurrying clouds that pressed lower and lower until they seemed to crowd the sea. The swells were rising and the great *Plutonic* lifted a little to their thrust, lifted with a faint rolling motion that forecast a heavy storm....

On the wings of the moaning wind, a burst of wild laughter echoed the length of the ship. A foreboding—that ever-fearful sense of horror and imminent evil—dragged cold fingers up Wentworth's spine. His automatic was back in its holster. With long loping strides, he raced toward that crazy mirth half the length of the ship away. He saw its source, a blurred, human figure, still shrieking senselessly as it mounted the rail. For a moment, the moon peered in fright through the tattered clouds, and for an instant, the scene was terribly clear. Clasped in each others arms, a man and woman were poised outside the rail!

A dozen voices caught up Wentworth's shout, terror and panic and warning joining in one vast, incoherent bedlam.

.. RICHARD WENTWORTH ..

People crowded into Wentworth's path. A woman running blindly struck him and recoiled, spinning against a stanchion, going down. A man shouted in fury, struck viciously at Wentworth with a deck chair. Wentworth dodged and ran on. When he could see again, the rail was empty of life.

"Man overboard!" he shouted. "Man overboard!"

As if his cry had been a signal, he saw another man climb to the rail. There could be no doubt of his intention. His movements were furtive: his backward glance, sly and gloating. He screamed his way outward into space and a tottering, aged woman struggled to the rail, also chuckling insanely.

Great God! Had the world gone mad? Wentworth shook his head savagely to clear it, rubbed a heavy hand across his forehead. Before this, he had seen mad scenes—criminals gone mad and killing like Seljuk Turks on a *djehad;* men writhing to death by a thousand foul means—but this utterly wild self-destruction—! He flung a haunted look about him. No, no, it was reality, not a nightmare.

That aged woman was still struggling to mount the rail. He dashed toward her and she spun on him like a cornered cat, spitting curses in a cracked, ancient voice, striking furiously with her rubber-tipped cane. A lurch of the ship threw her off balance and she pitched down, clutched frantically at the rail and struck her head. Well, she was safe…!

With set lips, Wentworth sprang to the rail, automatic in hand. "I'll shoot the next man or woman who tries to jump!" he shouted.

IT WAS as crazy as any part of the nightmare scene. What difference would lead make to a person suicide-bent? A gust of chill wind swept Wentworth, tugged at his coat as he stood, gripping a stanchion and waving the gun. Black smoke from the funnels swooped down upon the deck. For a moment, Wentworth was blinded. He opened his eyes in time to see a man creeping upon him with a foot-rack torn from a deck chair. He jerked it back over his head… There was only one thing to do.

Wentworth's gun cut a bloody gash in the darkness and the man's arm flopped limply, the chair clattered to the deck. He screamed and fled into the shadows. Twice more, Wentworth fired, burning lead along the rail. The people who avidly sought a death in the sea a moment before swept back from the ripping, bloody death of the Spider's lead. For fifteen long minutes, Wentworth kept his nightmare vigil there upon the rail. Then ship's officers and crew took charge and death-thirsty passengers were herded to their cabins and locked in.

Wentworth turned away heavily, wearily. No need to wait while the *Plutonic's* lifeboats combed the empty sea. His vital face was haggard and worn, but there was a hard grimness about it that erased the lines of care. His mouth was a straight, barren slit and his eyes held bitter, menacing lights. Standing by the rail, he deliberately reloaded his half-emptied automatic, watching the shadows, scrutinizing each officer that passed.

Recognizing him, they made no efforts to hinder him. They moved like men in a strange and hideous dream, but they went steadily about their duty. They were saved from madness by the necessity for action. But down in their cabins, hundreds of passengers had nothing to do but think of those who had died and to feel, perhaps, the germs of self-destruction grow, like the spores of some loathsome parasitic fungus, in their own brains.

Wentworth's horror was greater than theirs. He knew that such things could not happen simply from mass hysteria. There was some actuating force and motive behind all this, and that, undoubtedly, was human. How this devil's work was accomplished—the reasons behind it or what threatened next he did not know—but he knew where he would seek the answer. In the suite of Jamid Bey!

A soft step on the deck whipped his head about. Then he smiled, moved to meet Nita, crushing her hands in his lean, tanned fingers. They said nothing but looked deeply into each other's eyes. Then Wentworth led her along the deck toward the cabin she occupied with Mrs. Stanley, the aged woman who served her as companion and chaperone. No need for these two to speak of their joy in finding one another unaffected by the general mania. Theirs was a deep and understanding love, for all that it remained sterile in their breasts.

Some few moments they snatched out of the maelstrom of the Spider's life, but that was all. Even this leisurely trip back from the fjords of Norway must be interrupted by horror. In the midst of all this death, a new, old misery called him to his duty. There could never be more than this for them, a clinging of hands and a few sunny days together.

How could the Spider marry, beget children, be the loving husband and father when disgrace and death hung perpetually over his head? Wentworth had never swerved from his service to the people he loved, nor had he ever regretted his choice. But there were times when bitterness at his life rose to pinch his throat with hot fingers. And sometimes, as now, there was a cry in his soul: Must their love languish always amidst death and terror and nightmare crime?

At the door of her stateroom, the two paused a brief moment.

The soft white of Nita's gown merged with the darkness of her lover's clothes. A moment their lips and hearts clung together and then Wentworth was gone, a lean, striding figure in the dark.

As he circled toward the suite of the Egyptian, a far, faint suicide cry rose thinly into the night and the sound of it tightened Wentworth's mouth and soul. God grant that this might be one outburst of criminal malignance which he could scotch at its start and blast out of existence with his fiery guns.

By the gods, Jamid Bey would best talk well and swiftly!

## CHAPTER 3
## JAMID BEY

THE DOOR of Jamid Bey's suite opened at Wentworth's knock and one of the white-clad *fellaheen* who served the Egyptians bade him welcome with the fawning insolence of his kind, egg-shaped turbaned head hobbling on a long neck. With a single step that took him across the threshold, Wentworth entered another world. A strange, spicy incense came faintly to his nostrils and somewhere in the suite was the thin, archaic tinkling of some string instrument that was thumbed in an ancient rhythm.

Beneath Wentworth's feet, the carpet was thick. It did not take a close examination to know that the rich, deep red was that rarest of antique Barkhoum colors; that he trod on thousands of dollars. That did not surprise him, for he was used to a rich life, even to extravagance, but what was amazing was the enor-

mous changes that had been wrought in
this suite for a five-day cruise across the
Atlantic.

Exquisite tapestries were drawn aside
by the gaunt arm of the *fellah* and Wentworth strode into a room stripped of all
occidental significance.

Tapestries and even more rare carpets
covered the walls and floor, cushions
and three low divans, a table scarcely six

inches high, were the sole furnishings. Only the slow sway of
the draperies betrayed the fact that he was aboard a ship and not
in the intimate living quarters of an oriental home. Wentworth
was aware, without turning his head, of two huge blacks with
folded arms who stood on each side of the doorway, turbaned,
richly tunicked, with great bare scimitars thrust through their
sashes. But even more, he was aware of Nephtasu.

She knelt upon a cushion beside the low coffee-table and
greeted him with the lifting of her slant, green eyes and slow
smile of her slim and pale mouth.

"My uncle has asked me to greet you in his name," Nephtasu
murmured, "and to say that he will be with you shortly." Once
more the magic of her voice touched him—the subtle slurred
accent of the East.

Wentworth swept her in a single glance. The gorgeous gown
like the sea in the sun had been changed to a long, cloaked robe
of some shimmering, deep blue brocaded stuff, with a low V

throat and a collar that stood up stiffly to accent the grace of her slim throat. The belt was a slash of scarlet bound about the hips.

A slight smile was upon Wentworth's lips. So he was intended to be charmed? His bow was faultless. "Jamid Bey is pleased to be kind!"

He crossed to the table, sank down easily into the cross-legged sitting position which only those who have known and loved the East acquire. From a long-necked pot of bronze, Nephtasu poured coffee into white cups of incredibly thin porcelain.

"You have come to reproach me," she reproved gently. "I can see it in your eyes."

Wentworth trained his gaze upon the tiny coffee cup as he raised its black fragrance to his lips. He was intended to look into her hypnotic eyes, was he? Well…! The pleasure of battle flooded him with a deep warmth. The presence of the swordsmen was symbolic, for here was again the coldly evil presentiment of danger—the quivering sense of immense and fearsome things about to happen. His lifted brows were humorous.

"But my dear 'Tasu!" he demurred. "Surely it is your privilege to refuse a man's attentions! And every woman longs to have at least one suicide to her credit. No, I do not reproach you." He looked up now, suddenly, mockingly and caught the green flame of her eyes before she could veil them.

"You mock me!"

"Indeed no, 'Tasu."

He caught a whisper behind him, a few muttered words of Arabic. "Shall I kill now?" one swordsman whispered to the other. "He is insolent."

29

"There is to be a signal…!" the other rasped back.

THE MAN'S voice faded and Wentworth perceived that Nephtasu had moved her right hand sharply. His smile did not change, but the glint of his eyes was fiercer and gayer. So these two plotted his death? There was no longer any doubt then as to blame for the suicide wave. His vengeance must be swift and certain, but first he must learn the means that was used. There would be no trouble in disposing of bodies, Wentworth thought—but he was the Spider, now grim and inevitable as fate. These two had planned to toss his body into the sea and let it be assumed that he had killed himself as had so many others. Well, he was forewarned now, and Nephtasu was talking….

"As if no one had ever loved me before!" she cried. She knelt very erectly, almost as tall as Wentworth as he sat, her flaming hair more than ever a crown upon her head. And he saw that she played a part, too. There was no real indignation here; the contrition had been false too.

"I meant to imply none of that," Wentworth replied, "but the young chap seemed such poor game for a daughter of the Pharaohs. If she wished merely to see a man die, there are slaves, but…."

Ah, he had her there! The anger in those green eyes was genuine now and there was a hint of—by the gods, it was fear! She spoke with difficulty. "What do you mean… a daughter of the Pharaohs? What do you…?"

Wentworth leaned forward as her voice faltered. "Surely," he whispered, "surely one who comes wooing may be granted the privilege of hyperbole? You are very lovely, very much a princess...."

Contempt was in her eyes now, contempt... but Wentworth had seen the sway of curtains there against the wall. Now he rose easily to his feet, bowed politely to Jamid Bey.

There was a questioning flash in the man's imperious eyes as he glanced at the girl who knelt on the cushions. "Our guest's cup is empty!" he said smoothly.

"On the contrary," Wentworth bowed, lapsing into Arabic, "it hath been filled to overflowing!"

Wentworth caught the jerk of the girl's muscles, the involuntary flash of her eyes toward the two swordsmen at the door. She smiled up at him and murmured a phrase in a harsh, guttural tongue that seemed faintly familiar to Wentworth, but which he could not understand. One word he did catch, vaguely like the Arabic for uncle.

"Which means," said Nephtasu, "my thanks for a gracious word."

"I do not follow you there," Wentworth replied ruefully.

Jamid Bey said slowly. "She has ten tongues and each one is sharper than the one before."

Nephtasu filled the coffee cups, tendered one to each of the men and excused herself. The two men sat again and Wentworth took pains to keep the two swordsmen in partial view. He said conversationally:

"I'll have to trouble you, Jamid Bey, neither to look toward nor make any other sign that may be construed as a signal to the two at the door. If they begin a move toward me, I shall shoot you first."

Jamid Bey carried his cup to his lips, sipped appreciatively before he raised his gaze to Wentworth's. The eyes were black and cold and ruthless. He did not employ the futile subterfuge of denial.

"I rather fancied my ward's language trick did not escape you," he said and raised his voice in Arabic. "Leave our sight, dogs, and do not blacken it again. By thy loose prattling, thou hast placed us in deadly peril!"

WENTWORTH RECOGNIZED with a tightening of his watchful eyes, that Jamid Bey said *our* and *us,* knew that the man did not mean to include him in that pronoun, nor yet Nephtasu. It was a veritable royal *we!* He remembered the start of surprise—and perhaps terror—when he had called the girl a daughter of the Pharaohs. The devil! Did these two consider themselves the imperial descendants of the long dynasties of Egypt?

He noted the stiff-backed penitence of the two with swords; their faces drained of life. Jamid Bey turned carelessly to his coffee cup, but Wentworth had a glimpse of his black gaze before the two men, marching as on parade, crossed the room and, pulling aside a rug, stepped out onto the private deck.

"Now we may talk," said Bey.

Wentworth was straining his ears. He thought it barely possible that the exit of the two might be a ruse to attack him with some weapon more effective at a distance than a sword. He thought he heard faintly a splash, but he could not be sure.

The wind was rising and made a low mourning about the decks.

Jamid Bey slowly refilled the coffee cups. "I feel that I owe you an explanation, sir," he said easily. There was no true apology in his voice, no warning of the cold, commanding eyes, "but, too, you might be called on for explanation, coming armed into the home of a friend."

Wentworth acknowledged that with a slow, stiff nod of his head. "Yet it seems that I did well not to trust too much in your—hospitality."

Jamid Bey's back had stiffened as Wentworth hesitated over his final word, but he relaxed a little. An imputation against his hospitality he might pass over, but never against his honor.

"A precaution," he lifted the cup to his lips. "Purely a precautionary measure. I do not know precisely what you heard those dogs say, but it is the truth that they were not to act without a signal. After all, sir, you were armed on the deck a little earlier tonight and showed some rare skill with your weapon…."

Wentworth controlled himself with an effort. Some member of Jamid Bey's suite had seen him shooting. The dim figure in white that had fled his bullets and leaped overboard came back to his mind. Damn! Could that not have been one of the *fellaheen* in his white robe? It was difficult to force his mind back to Jamid Bey's words:

"It was not inconceivable," the Egyptian was saying, "that after last night's demonstration of hypnotism and my ward's foolish romanticism on the boat-deck, you might become suspicious. I understand that in your own country you have rather a formidable reputation as an amateur criminologist."

When he had finished, Jamid Bey set down his cup with a steady hand, placed a palm on each of his folded knees. "I make this explanation in justice to you." His voice harshened, deepened became a singing challenge. "But I make no apology. If you require further satisfaction, there are ways of giving or receiving it."

Wentworth's lips curved slightly. Here was no *braggadocio*. The man would perform willingly what he had implied—a duel of any description—if Wentworth made any criticism of his honor. But the explanation had been handsomely made and the man had been entirely justified—if he told the truth. Wentworth lifted his gray-blue eyes, sustained the piercing cold of that black, arrogant gaze. The hawkish face was imperious. It was impossible to consider falsehood or fear in connection with the lean hardness behind that mask. This was a man to Wentworth's liking, he found amazingly, nor could he find distrust in his heart despite his suspicion of a moment before. After all, the presence of one of this man's slaves on the companion-way did not involve either man or master necessarily. But obviously, he could accomplish nothing by direct challenge. His certainty of the man's guilt was dissipating....

SLOWLY WENTWORTH lifted his right hand to his gun, drew the weapon and offered it to Jamid Bey, butt first. "There can be no dishonor," he said gently, "where none is intended."

A spark of admiration leaped into the other's black eyes. With a courteous gesture, Jamid Bey declined the weapon and Wentworth placed it on the floor between them. For a long moment afterward, the two men gazed, eye to eye, mind to mind. Then slowly the Egyptian nodded.

"I tender my apologies, sir," he said slowly. "It is a thing I am not accustomed to do and I perform it awkwardly. But I perceive I have done you an injustice."

"Speak no more of it, Jamid Bey."

Wentworth's brow was clear, but there was worry and wonder in his brain. It was not his habit to jump at conclusions and even Jamid Bey admitted the justice of his suspicions in this case. Wentworth had known gentlemen who were criminals before this, but he could not, facing this man, accuse him of perfidy. Yet Wentworth was more convinced than ever of human agency behind the wave of suicides—the peculiar actions of men and women fighting for the privilege of dying. Jamid Bey had acknowledged similar thoughts in his explanation of his precautions.

"You, too," Jamid Bey broke in on his thoughts, "are convinced of a human agency behind these deaths?" It was not actually a question, but rather a statement of fact which courtesy prohibited making a declaration.

"No question of it," Wentworth said slowly, recognizing with a nod the other's ability at mental telepathy. He knew something of it himself, could practice it on occasion. "No question at all. But the means employed are somewhat obscure. I'll admit I had suspected hypnotism, especially when I was certain that during the demonstration you concealed the greater part of your ability." Wentworth tried to force himself to an open-minded discussion, but his mind remained tight with suspicions. He felt, too, that there was peril near for him—deadly overwhelming peril—though he could not persuade himself now that it emanated from Bey.

Jamid Bey acknowledged the correctness of his observation on his hypnotic demonstration. "You are shrewd as well as honorable, sir."

"However," Wentworth continued, "tonight I saw two persons, one dead, the other attempting suicide, whom I know positively to have not been present nor to have come in contact with you in any way. I would guess now that something has been introduced into the food or water supply, or that some maddening gas has been circulated in the ventilation system."

Jamid Bey sat silent for long moments. It was apparent that he was deep in thought. Once he raised his eyes to those of his guest. Then he shook his head abruptly. "I cannot obtain the answer tonight," he said slowly, "or, I'm afraid, anywhere at sea. Would you do me the honor of calling upon me at the Carlston, say two days after landing?"

Wentworth rose easily to his feet. Jamid Bey picked up his automatic and handed it to him, smiling with his thin, almost colorless lips.

"A cigarette on deck before you go?" he suggested.

Wentworth acquiesced with a bow. They lighted long, thin Egyptians from a box of ancient carved ivory and strolled together toward the carpeted wall. Jamid Bey went first, brushing aside the rugs and Wentworth smiled slightly. He went first to disprove the taint of treachery. But Wentworth was tortured by uncertainty. He was positive that Jamid Bey had attempted, sitting silently there before him, to commune with some source about revealing information. There was no doubt about it. Wentworth himself did not give telepathy so much credit.

IT COULD not have been the girl, Nephtasu, with whom he sought to communicate or there would be no need to delay until they were ashore. Jamid Bey's attitude had been almost one of prayer, eyes closed, body at rest. After all, prayer might be considered a form of telepathy, he supposed. Perhaps the ancients actually had communed with God in that way, receiving their answer in a sort of benign glow or sensation of happiness… Wentworth felt a cold touch of—almost of fear. He whirled on Jamid Bey.

"Two nights ago," he said sharply, "I received a warning."

Jamid Bey smiled curiously. "You are gifted, my friend. It was on that night that I, too, received the warning. When you played that strange music, I wondered. Yes, I wondered greatly."

Wentworth moved his shoulders impatiently. This was absurd, of course. To consider it possible that some omniscient, benign influence had warned him of danger to come and had, apparently, warned Jamid Bey in more detail! It was even sillier to think that the harshened, throbbing music from his violin had been distantly inspired. Especially why—if there really was such an influence—should it be Egyptian? Might it not as well be Chinese, or for that matter, Ethiopian? But the fact remained that from the hour when the strange music came from his violin as if in spite of him he had sensed an evil foreboding....

They were standing at the rail now, staring out over the wind-tumbled seas that raced off to leeward, white gaps gleaming ghostly in the smother of clouds and spray. The *Plutonic* was lumbering at reduced speed, climbing and twisting gigantically. The private deck, on the leeward side, was screened in by tight barriers that fitted solidly to deck, an overhead canopy on each side... Suddenly, Wentworth frowned. The two armed blacks! Where were they?

He flung a swift glance about, but there was no trace of the two, nor was there any place they might have gone. An abruptly rigidity swelled his shoulder muscles, tautened his neck. That splash he had heard just after the two left the room. Jamid Bey had said: "Leave our sight and never blacken it again!" Wentworth whirled about stiffly, met the cold, unmoved smile of Jamid Bey. There was a new sharpness to his hawk's face, a more imperious lift of his head.

"My house," he said clearly, but slowly, as if he had difficulty now in speaking English, "does not tolerate inadequate... servants."

## CHAPTER 4
## THE MAN-MOUNTAIN

WENTWORTH CONTROLLED himself with an effort, curious instead of shocked about Jamid Bey's calm execution by suicide of his two sword-bearers. It was probably, too, that the white-robed man whom Wentworth had shot had been badly wounded and jumped overboard rather than bring suspicion upon his master. It was exceedingly strange that the Bey's men were executed by suicide… Jamid Bey became increasingly aloof so Wentworth shortly took his leave. Each of them exchanging courtesies as the door was opened.

With the perpetual caution which had often saved him before, Wentworth flung a quick glance up and down the corridor as he stepped out. His movements thereafter were as swift as the automatic that leaped to his hand.

"Back, Jamid Bey!" he cried.

He himself did the reverse of the expected. Instead of checking his advance and retreating, he saved wasted motion and time by plunging forward in a dive. As he went across the corridor, he twisted toward the lurking assassin he had spotted in the shadows. Two guns blasted together, but Wentworth's move had confused his assailant. His heavy gun barked then he caught himself with an out-thrown hand, got his feet under him, lunged to the attack….

The ambusher had reared up stiffly where he crouched, back arching painfully, gun hand rising without direction. Wentworth straightened, relaxing. His automatic was already in its holster when the man went limp and slammed down on his face.

"Well done, sir," came the quiet voice of Jamid Bey at his side. "But for your cry, that bullet would have taken me in the temple, or between the eyes. I thank you."

Wentworth nodded curtly, knelt, rolled over the man he had killed. His ears were still ringing from the blast of the gun in the

confined space and the Egyptian's words were heard dimly. A glance at the man's face and Wentworth got to his feet stiffly, frowning. It was the same man who had attacked him on deck and through whose arm he had put a bullet. He identified the man briefly to Jamid Bey, then at once took his leave as ship officers came racing.

Wentworth's eyes were narrowed and thoughtful as he went through the identification of the dead man. As soon as possible, he hurried to his suite, watching keenly the shadows and corridors about him. It was after two o'clock in the morning and, when the door was closed behind him, he realized he was suddenly weary. Ram Singh moved toward him on bare silent feet, offering a tall glass of heavily laced *café royal*. Wentworth took it gratefully, began talking to Ram Singh in brief snatches of Hindustani as he detailed what had happened and what threatened.

He was troubled by his involuntary trust of the enigmatic Egyptian—still more puzzled by the man's apparent occult powers. The ruthlessness with which he had disposed of the "inadequate" servants, who were indubitably slaves, was typical of course, if indeed he did come from the royal blood of the Pharaohs. What troubled Wentworth even more was the attack in the corridor. He considered it extremely unlikely now that Jamid Bey had been behind the deadly rifleman who had so nearly slain him in the ocean. He must seek elsewhere for the sponsor of that assassin. The motive was obscure, unless it was necessary to the plotter that the man he had rescued should die.

With the thought, Wentworth came sharply from the comfortable chair into which he had sunk.

"With me, Ram Singh!"

HE STRODE to the door with the dry whisper of the loyal Hindu's feet behind him, hurried through deserted, hushed corridors to the sick bay. The doctor, bearded and cheerful, looked up at Wentworth briskly. "Well, what's wrong with you, young fellow? Feel any inclination toward suicide?"

Wentworth smiled at him. "Young fellow, yourself, you scamp! How are you, Masters?"

The doctor came to his feet. "Major Wentworth! Dick Wentworth! Damn, man, I didn't recognize you. I haven't seen you since—"

"The Argonne," Wentworth said grimly, "and you did a damnably painful job of extracting a shrapnel ball from my left bicep."

"No anesthetics," Dr. Masters apologized, looking him over slowly. "Fit as ever except you sleep too little. God, man, I'll never forget the day I excised that ball. You cursed me like a sergeant for telling you to take blighty, went back into it again."

"I managed to carry the objective, you know." Wentworth was growing impatient with the chit-chat, "and the machine guns had my boys stopped dead. Oh, well."

"Single-handed, you did, and only a lieutenant, then." Masters grumbled. "Why in the hell do you pull that modesty stuff on me. You got a medal, the *Legion*…."

*"Officer,"* Wentworth confirmed. "They gave me the *Chevalier* before that at Château Thierry. I'm a commander now, and I also have the D.S.O. and the *croix de guerre* with assorted palms, but not the Victoria Cross. Now for heaven's sake, will that satisfy you? I want to get on with business."

Masters grunted, continued to peer at Wentworth without words.

"The man who went overboard. How is he?"

"You mean the *men.*"

"Well, the first one, then...."

"All right," Masters said disgustedly. "I had to work on him for over half an hour, artificial respiration, before he came around. And that damned Stuyvesant girl stood around with tears running down her cheeks and wouldn't be put out. By the great oath of Hippocrates! I'll bet you're the one saved him!"

"Get me the Carnegie medal for that, will you, doc?" Wentworth said mockingly. "Now look here. What's the man's name and where is he?"

"Denver Dane, believe it or not," Masters was groping in his pockets, "and he's in B-56." He got out a cigar and bit off the end. "And the girl's still with him." He looked up from lighting his cigar, talking out smoke, but Wentworth was gone.

Ram Singh knocked at Dane's cabin, then stood with folded arms, eyes questing up and down the corridor. The door opened a crack and a girl's black, curly head showed. She stared at Wentworth for a long moment, then suddenly flung the door wide and threw both arms about his neck.

"Oh, it's *you!*" she cried. "You! If it hadn't been for you,

Denvie would be dead now. I—I—" She was crying suddenly. Catching Wentworth's hand, she pulled him into the cabin. Behind them, Ram Singh closed the door and Wentworth knew that he took up his stand outside, hands never far from the nine-inch throwing-knives hidden always beneath his clothing.

The man on the bunk was bedraggled, blond hair sprawling from his lolling head, but there was something queer about his eyes. Wentworth saw that this was because the brows slanted upward at the outer ends. He had a weak, self-indulgent mouth.

"Denvie, this is the man who saved you," the girl told him enthusiastically. "Damn, I forgot to ask your name!"

Wentworth gave his name, and smiling, shook hands to ease the boy's obvious embarrassment.

"Silly stunt I pulled." Denver Dane said pleasantly. "Awfully decent of you going into the wet for me."

WENTWORTH DROPPED into a chair while the girl sat on the foot of the berth and kept her bright, dark gaze roving from one face to the other like the eyes of an excited young puppy with two masters equally beloved. The girl was very young, Wentworth saw, but there was good stuff in her. The carriage was fine, the small, shapely head high and haughty on occasion. There was intelligence in the well-formed nose and square-set eyes. She still wore the fluffy evening dress of white, ruined now with salt water stains.

"Anybody on board that doesn't go for you in a big way, Dane?" Wentworth asked quietly.

Dane made a wry face. "Sure. Mr. Stuyvesant isn't so hot for me but the Mrs. makes him keep me on. And I think I make a big squash where the gypsy girl was concerned."

Wentworth shook his head impatiently, smiling slightly at the word gypsy as applied to Nephtasu. "I mean anyone who would want to kill you?"

Dane's eyes bulged large. "Good lord, no!"

The girl reached out a hand to Wentworth's arm. "What is it?"

"Know any secrets worth being killed over?"

Dane laughed nervously. "Mr. Stuyvesant doesn't trust me with anything big and outside of that… no, nothing!"

Wentworth leaned back in the chair, eyes brooding. He had hoped that he might uncover some trail here that would lead to the persons responsible for the suicide, but if Dane held the clue, he seemed unaware of it. His answers had been spontaneous, clearly truthful.

It was, of course, possible that he had seen or heard something, unimportant, which later might prove incriminating to those that had said it. But even of that Wentworth was dubious.

He posted Ram Singh to keep watch over those who came to the cabin and went alertly back to his staterooms. A short man of quick impatient movements was pacing jerkily up and down before the door. At sight of Wentworth, he sprang toward him, hands reaching out, eyes bulging excitedly.

"At last! At last!" he cried. "I thought you never were going to return. Listen, you must be interested. You must, and I imag-

44

ine you will be, for—" he paused impressively—"I know who you are!"

He emphasized the words with a lean forefinger tapping against Wentworth's chest. Wentworth took the hand and put it aside with a quiet smile on his lips, but his mind was racing. This man could not mean that he knew his secret identity as the Spider. No, that was impossible. Certainly, if he did, he would take no such way as this to reveal his knowledge. But what, then, did the man mean?

"Very good of you," Wentworth said stiffly.

The little man took two quick steps away, then back. "You're Richard Wentworth," he said accusingly, "the great criminologist! And you're not doing a thing to stop these mad suicides. Or are you—are you? I couldn't make absolutely sure whether you were deliberating some preventive activity or whether you were merely remaining passive. Yes, that's it. That's it!"

THE MAN'S face worked as rapidly as his mouth in delivering his hurried, strangely long-winded speeches. The eyes were enthusiastic, glittering behind horn-rimmed spectacles. He moved constantly, arms, legs, even his body.

"I should know you," Wentworth said, slowing his speech deliberately. "I've seen you with that superb artist, Craft Elliott."

"Of course you have. Of course. I'm glad to see that you realize the worth of that great genius. He is a truly marvelous artist and those critics who do not approve of his school are negligible men—negligible men! One stroke of his brush, ahhh! But pardon me, I'm afraid that I have failed to identify myself in the rush of my enthusiasm for this great master whom I serve.

Sneed Jenkins, agent of art, and especially of Elliott's art, at your service, sir."

He executed a ducking, absurd little bow like the bobbing of a snipe on a sandbank, and immediately was talking again, faster than ever:

"Mr. Elliott has some marvelous plans for preventing this wholesale suicide from continuing. He sent me especially to petition you to visit him. You'll pardon the imposition of requesting your presence at such an hour, requesting your presence at all. Elliott would come to you, indeed he would. The great Wentworth! But he is, as you undoubtedly know, somewhat sensitive about his excess of weight. He is, for a fact. He detests going anywhere where people can see him and gape at him. He says it makes his work seem ridiculous, to know that fat

JAMID BEY

CRAFT ELLIOTT

SNEED JENKINS

46

NEPHTASU

CAPTAIN
JORGENSEN

JACKSON
GRANT

fingers, terribly fat fingers that scarcely seem able to grip a brush, committed anything to canvas."

Wentworth stared at the little man curiously but with alert eyes, keeping a watch on the corridor at the same time. Death had struck at him many times tonight....

"I'd be glad to talk with Mr. Elliott at any time about anything," Wentworth said slowly. "He has undoubted genius. That bit of his called, now let me see—yes, simply *Chiaroscuro*—that exquisite thing done almost with the fineness of etching...."

Sneed Jenkins beamed all over his absurd, puckered, little face at the praise of his principal. He pranced about, shifting from foot to foot.

"Glad you liked it. Glad. Very glad! Now, Mr. Wentworth, you will come with me at once, will you not? It is so terribly, so vitally important that the only really great minds concerned with this problem get together at once and pool their mental resources for the suppression of this huge and monstrous thing which has...."

Wentworth looked longingly at his door, warily along the corridor, then walked off beside the chattering magpie of an agent whom Craft Elliott used superfluously to market his rare works. The man's employment found its source in the sensitiveness that Sneed Jenkins had mentioned, his immense fatness, so great that his awkward body was almost unmaneuverable in ordinary houses. It was a marvel that his giant hands could achieve such artistry....

Wentworth's caution did not desert him for a minute. He was convinced that the man who had waylaid him at Jamid Bey's door had been inspired by the rifleman who so nearly sent him to the bottom of the sea. The wounded man, crazed as he had been earlier, would have made an easy subject for the persuasion of an intelligent man, and in his condition, would never have been able to track Wentworth down as he had.

Wentworth did not trust even this comical little popinjay with his absurd mannerisms and his minutely careful clothing. Tragedy before this, had hid behind a laughing mask. Wentworth jeered at himself—*laugh clown, laugh!*—but his eyes continued to watch the shadows.

CRAFT ELLIOTT'S stateroom was full of shadows. In the midst of the biggest, blackest one sat the artist. Wentworth had known that Elliott was enormously fat, had expected to find a large man. But he was stunned, made almost physically sick by the sight of the immense creature who sat there in the half darkness that obviously was another, sop to his sensitiveness. It seemed almost obscene to say that this man sat, except in the sense that a building sits upon its foundations or a pyramid upon the sands. He overwhelmed the chair.

Pendulous laps reposed on his thighs and swelled outward beyond his knees. His head seemed a small button with the sagging balloons of his cheeks attached and his hands... Wentworth rigidly forced himself to cease taking stock of this monstrosity before him and bowed suavely. "I knew you were aboard, Mr. Elliott, and had longed for the privilege of meeting the man who could do a thing like your *chiaroscuro*," he said. "Yours is a great genius."

Elliott said, "Nonsense!" His voice was high, thin, squeezed out with wheezing breath. Wentworth wondered how the heart could continue the incredible labor of supplying that colossal girth with blood. He had a momentary imaginary picture of a heart, swollen with fat also, pumping out fat blood... He had to stop that sort of thing or he *would* be sick. It was the fatigue, he told himself.

"Nonsense!" Elliott wheezed. "Appreciative though. Nice bit. Another purpose in calling you. Suicides." Wentworth saw that he conserved words to save breath for his body. He remembered the etching-like fineness of the work they both had mentioned and, in the gloom, had a glimpse of the man's arm and hand, the wrist almost thigh-size, the hand, even the fingers, padded with little swollen balloons of fat. When he painted or drew, he must wheeze like a bellows. Suppose a man had elephantiasis of the foot and leg and then tried to paint with it? It would be equivalent. A poisonous, fungoid man. Wentworth was not given to emotionalism, certainly not about the appearance of a man, but he had a feeling that the stateroom was loathsomely crowded and that he must escape soon. He could not any longer stand here and listen to the man's tortured breathing. He was offered a chair, but declined, still politely, saying that he was very weary and must hurry back to sleep… if he had sat, that mountain of flesh would have toppled over upon him and smothered him….

As soon as was decently possible, Wentworth left, Sneed Jenkins bouncing along at his side. They were on their way to the captain's quarters to do what Wentworth had planned for the morning, to inaugurate a series of recreational features which might divert passengers' minds from the impulse to self-destruction.

The captain assented ungraciously to their admittance and stood, lank and tall, with his head bowed as if to protect it from many low ceilings and doorways. He had a dour, long, lined face and bristling hair which marched down to a low point on his forehead.

"Damned silliness!" he said gruffly when they had proposed their plan. "If the damned incompetents want to dispose of themselves, why not permit it?"

Wentworth was familiar with the dour captain's pedantic manner of speech at the dinner table. A peculiar man, well educated, yet strenuous and hard with the old manner of the sea. Captain Jorgensen was quite old. This was in fact his retiring trip, and with the landing at New York, he would leave the sea forever, at least so far as command was concerned. He turned, stalked to his desk, jabbed a bell button indignantly. A steward popped in through a door with the quickness of a weasel in a way that spoke marvels for the captain's discipline.

"Mr. Mixon," Jorgensen growled. "Refreshments."

He spun back to Wentworth, ignoring the bouncing, grimacing Jenkins.

"Mind you, Wentworth," he said. "I don't think these specious entertainments will militate one iota against suicidal mania. But since an old acquaintance of mine requests it and this is my retiring voyage—Mixon will attend to it. By the way, Wentworth—" Jorgensen walked toward him, long-legged as a crane. "—if your first voyage is called a maiden trip, you could devise quite a disreputable nomenclature for the last, eh? Eh?" He laughed, a single explosive: *"Ha!"* That was all; then his face was dour and long-lined again.

"Jenkins, you would best return to the reposing place of Man-Mountain Elliott and assure him that the suicidal mania shall not afflict him. Which—" he turned to Wentworth as Jenkins faded into the background and slipped in a whipped-dog way out of the door—"which is, after all, the sole thing that quakes in the breast of the Man-Mountain." He made a wry face. "I don't often have obscene thoughts, Wentworth, truly I don't, but about that monstrosity… *Ha!* Listen, Wentworth—" two lean fingers caught him by the lapel, "—If Elliott is a mountain, d'y'see, and a laugh is an earthquake."

## CHAPTER 5
## WHEN A GOD COMMANDS

**W**ENTWORTH HAD some further suggestions to make to the captain. They concerned guarding the food supplies against adulteration, keeping a watch over the water and the ventilation system. He stayed with Captain Jorgensen an hour longer while these things were done and then he refused a final drink and prepared to go. He had his own plans. When he had caught up on his sleep, he wanted to find an expert rifleman or at least a telescope, target rifle.

"Have a cigar, Wentworth," urged Jorgensen. "Very excellent cigars. I can recommend them with perfect equanimity."

"Sorry, no thanks, captain. I'm very tired."

"I know you must be—must be! That rescue today, tonight it was. Finest thing I ever saw...."

Jorgensen's head was swaying a little from side to side, his eyes shifty and hot and suddenly he was snarling filthy abuse.

"I'm glad they're dead," he cried with a muffled fury worse than screams. "Every damned one that jumps over the rail, I'll cheer. By God, *cheer!* Piddling nasty little passengers, cluttering up a sailin' man's ship..." He came two tottering steps forward. "For God's sake, Wentworth, don't leave me. Every pop-eyed dead man's face will resurrect itself to float about my head until I go mad." He swung a great raw-boned fist in a wide, vicious circle. "Damn you! I never could tolerate levitation!"

Wentworth rang for the steward. "Put the captain to bed, steward. He is... not well."

Jorgensen hurled his glass and a thick curse at the steward but the man came forward warily. "Sorry, captain, sir. Representative's orders. You're to go to bed. Really sir," he explained aside to Wentworth, "he's been on duty almost forty hours. It's simply fatigue, sir."

Wentworth, pacing the deck, wary-eyed toward his stateroom and sleep at last, computed with a puzzled frown that the captain's forty hours dated from the moment when—when the warning had come to Jamid Bey and to himself! Bathing, dragging on silken pajamas, Wentworth dropped to the side of his bed and stared at the wall. Gods above! This horror was bad enough here on board ship, where there was some chance of controlling it, but suppose it got loose in New York City! Suppose this strange virus, gas, drug, whatever it was, spread progressively across the nation!

A groaned curse forced itself between Wentworth's set lips. Very deliberately, he considered whether he should slip to Jamid Bey's quarters and kill him, print on his forehead the small red Spider seal that would claim him prey of justice. But, damn it, he couldn't be *certain*. When he was with the man, he was confident Bey was incapable of such fiendishness—and besides there were others equally open to suspicions. There was the captain with his rabid curses. Hell, one might as well suspect Man-Mountain Elliott of tiptoeing around the decks whispering suicide into unsuspecting ears. Or Stuyvesant, father of that black-haired girl who idolized the weak-mouthed youngster he had saved from the sea.

Elliott, too, had spoken of his fears of forty hours before, which, actually, was the only sound basis for suspicion of Jamid Bey, except that Nephtasu had prompted the first suicidal attempt. Wentworth dropped his head into his hand, squeezed the temples between his palms. He was being ridiculous. He could not go around killing all suspects in the hope he might get the right one. Perhaps no one was guilty... but he didn't believe that....

WENTWORTH FELL back across his bed, slept heavily until a repeated soft rapping at the door awakened him and Nita called softly that it was almost noon....

But there would have been no use in rising earlier. Nor did the next, dragging day and the sleepless night that followed bring results. Seven persons committed suicide in the first mad stampede and fourteen more sought quick, black death before the twenty-four hours were out. They hanged themselves to ventilator-registers, shot themselves and opened veins with razor blades. One athletic youth even climbed the foremast and plunged head-first to the deck. It seemed a macabre field-day of death, in which men and women vied with hell in the enormity of their crimes against themselves.

The rails were guarded, and after the morning roll showed many vacancies, a search was made for instruments which might inflict injuries. And all the while Wentworth sought that telescope rifle, vainly as he had feared.

Men and women were compelled to surrender everything with a sharp point or an edge that might cut the flesh. They overlooked matches and one woman set herself afire after wrapping bedding and mattress tightly about her. Wentworth was with the doctor when he injected an overdose of morphine to end her agony.

"It would be better," he said bitterly, "if Captain Jorgensen would line the whole damned ship-load up against the rail and give the order... *alley oop!*" Doctor Masters was haggard-eyed, his natural ruddiness drained away.

Wentworth did not look at him, but at his trembling hands. He was reflecting that doctors knew of many curious drugs. This one might have found a drug that would exterminate a ship-load of people by suicide. But why? In heaven's name, why? Men do not wipe out their fellow creatures simply for a lark. Religion or hatred or money in any one of its myriad forms. For these men killed wholesale. Sometimes—but rarely—for love.

Wentworth spoke flatly, dully: "You'll be rid of all this within another twelve hours. I'll be with it to the end, until the people behind it have answered for their crimes."

"People behind it!" Masters stared at Wentworth, laughed shortly. "Come on and have a drink. This thing is getting you."

FOR TWELVE, for twenty-four hours after the *Plutonic* drew her death-haunted steel plates up to the dock—while the newspapers still howled the frantic mystery of the twenty-seven men and women suicides—Wentworth sought through fatigue-ridden hours to trace the thing that caused these deaths. The newspapers, scientists, offered no solution. They spoke of mass suggestion and cited records....

But Wentworth knew. He sought, too, for the record of someone of the men who was an expert rifleman. Jamid Bey wasn't, but one of his men might well be. It was not that Wentworth wanted so vitally to find his assailant, but the man must be closely tied up with what had followed. He understood now that the rifleman had cared nothing about him, personally, but had sought to give the suicide suggestion a strong emphasis. A double death would have served excellently....

Wentworth's watch over Denver Dane had revealed no further attempt on his life and this materially influenced Wentworth's opinion.

But when twenty-four hours had passed, the suicide toll of New York City began its upward climb. There are always four, five, or six such deaths daily, but now that figure became seventy. On the following day, two-hundred sixty-four men and women killed themselves. Subways were jammed for long hours by maddened people who hurled themselves to ghastly death under the trucks. A series of suicides leaped from high bridges, from the towering peaks of skyscrapers. A truck-driver ran amuck with his loaded machine and smashed through a half-dozen loaded automobiles before he snuffed out his life by driving off a viaduct.

WENTWORTH WAS tortured by uncertainties and worries. Never before had a mass attack upon the country found him struggling so futilely for something against which to battle. Scores died daily under the suicide scourge of some megalomaniac criminal and the Spider—defender of distressed humanity—was helpless!

Nita was never far from his side these grave hours, save when, in grimy disguise, he sought in the Underworld some clue to the identity of the person behind these fierce ravagings—some logical motive. Among the blowsy, drink-sodden human dregs, the virus of self-destruction seemed not to strike; but neither was there any significant news. Wentworth found suspicion rife, but none *knew* anything and the Spider could guess more accurately than they.

Wentworth had even spied secretly on Denver Dane and as many other members of the ship party as he could reach, but all active leads failed to give him a definite, usable clue. His personal vigilance never relaxed. The rifle attack had been as impersonal as fate; but that other, the shot at Jamid Bey's door…!

It was best to take no chances.

From the first day when reporters had thronged aboard the doom ship. Wentworth had issued statements that the deaths were man-caused. He reminded them that suicides had been one of ten plagues of ancient Egypt. Deliberately he was baiting the enemy to attack him, hoping for the visit of an assassin….

The city began a campaign of free entertainments, sponsored, Wentworth saw with amusement, by the fat artist's agent. Sneed Jenkins. The man appeared, eagerly smiling, energetically speaking, in talking motion pictures and on the front pages of newspapers. And the same day he pronounced his entertainments a certain cure, six-hundred and forty-five men and women committed suicide.

THAT WAS the day before the night when Anubis—Egypt's god of darkness and death—came wrathfully to visit Wentworth…!

Wentworth had flung himself down upon his bed late at night and dropped immediately into an exhausted sleep. Fatigue, worry, the weariness of utter futility gripped him. Never before had the Spider been so conscious of sweeping, overpowering forces of evil, and yet been completely unable to cope with them. It was not that they were so mighty, but because they simply did not seem to exist!

Even Nita's presence, or the usually soothing strains of his precious violin, had no power to assuage his sterile wrath and his bitter anger at himself for being unable to solve the problem and find at least some minor agent of the death-syndicate against whom to battle. He was haunted especially by the news of one terrific suicide pact. A score of young men and women had killed themselves that afternoon in the middle of Park Avenue. A traffic policeman had seen them first, a block away, the leader carrying a wooden box in his hands. He suspected some soap-box speaking and started leisurely forward to interrupt.

He was still a half-block away when the group started to sing. The dirge had a mournful, weird sound—and then the officer saw a sputtering spark which he recognized as a lighted fuse. The policeman darted forward bravely, piping on his whistle, shouting—but before he had run a dozen paces, there came a terrific concussion and giddy blackness for the officer.

Not one of the dead was identifiable. Only one girl, who was blown through a window the width of the street away, lived more than a moment after the blast….

**IT WAS** fantastically horrible and Wentworth, who had gone to the scene, had urged his friend, Commissioner Flynn of the police, to learn something about the song the suicides had chanted. It seemed the only tangible clue, for not one of the dead could be identified and hence no questions asked of friends or relatives about their activities.

Flynn shook his long, hard head stubbornly, so Wentworth pursued the lead alone. He found one man, a teacher of violin music, whose window looked down on the scene of death, marked now by a jagged pit in the pavement of Park Avenue. The sound of massed chanting voices had drawn him to the window and he had looked out in time to see the explosion. He had caught only four minor notes and, as he played them, something that was vaguely familiar stirred Wentworth strangely. The violinist thought he could use the four notes as motif for a song, something like *Chloe*....

All this was fine preparation for the visit of a god of darkness—and death!

Wentworth had been sleeping lightly in spite of his fatigue. Suddenly he was lying there on the bed tensely, every nerve taut, every sense alert. His hands closed upon his ever-present guns, holstered on each side of the bed. Slowly, elaborately cautious, he studied every inch of his dark room. A mild breeze kited at the window curtains, and its coolness—the dense blackness outside—told him the hot August dawn could not be far off.

Yet, save for the silent swaying of the drapery, nothing moved. Wentworth slid his legs to the floor, and bare-footed, crept to the door. Ram Singh reared in a silent salaam, sleeping on the threshold as he often did in time of danger. Wentworth breathed a query, but the faithful Hindu had heard or seen nothing—absolutely nothing. With tedious caution, the two made a complete circuit of the fifteen room duplex in which

Wentworth lived. They searched everywhere—even the terrace outside, but there was absolutely nothing which could have given the alarm. Yet, Wentworth had been awakened, tense and alert, by something!

He returned to his bed, but sleep would not come. Finally he arose with a tired heaviness in his limbs and head, donned a brocaded robe that had come from a Chinese emperor's wardrobe and felt-sole, silken slippers. He went slowly down the graceful, circular stairs to his study below, through that to his music room. Moodily he crossed to his violin, trailing his finger tips over its matchless surface. He could not say why he had come. It had been days since he had touched bow to strings, but now he felt a sudden urge to play.

He tucked the instrument under his chin, and without preliminary, brushed out the four notes that the suicides had chanted before they died. They were somber, and their minor wail seemed to deepen the shadows of the room. Wentworth's eyes closed and he repeated them softly, deliberately, and slowly began to play.

At first, his notes were hesitant and uncertain, but presently they strengthened and the four notes grew into music, mournful and measured, somehow sentient with evil—like an incantation to some awful, loathsome demon. Wentworth felt cold seep into his veins and crawl over him like moist slow slugs. His bowing became more vigorous and sweeping until the damnable sound and rhythm of the thing filled the vaulted room tremendously. Wentworth's eyes were locked shut. Impossible to open them. It wasn't allowed....

Wentworth repeated that phrase in his brain. *It wasn't allowed!* What the hell was he talking about? He opened his eyes and the bow fell idle on the strings.

He stood, stiff and motionless, staring at a single spot on the dark wainscoting. He had to twist his head about to see it, but somehow he knew that was the place.

Ah, yes, that was the spot, for there was a glow there—a glow that strengthened with a steady pulsing light until it took on the nebulous outlines of a figure and then....

Wentworth breathed out hoarsely between his teeth; violin and bow came down—the bow like a sword in his hand. He could feel the pounding of his pulse like some great temple-drum; then his heart gave a high leap and stood still, trembling. Against the dark wall of the room *stood a man!*

THERE COULD be no doubt at all about it. Why he even threw a shadow there on the floor! But he was oddly dressed; his sternly muscled chest, red as bronze, was bare. His clothing was a stiff, archaic, paneled skirt and upon the head was set a striped, cloth head-dress. These things Wentworth observed quite calmly as if it were an everyday matter for an ancient Egyptian to materialize in his music room. Then his eyes lifted to the face and the bow fell from his hand. He saved the violin only by a frantic effort. The face—the face had a long, pointed nose, dog teeth and lolling tongue—Good lord! It was a *jackal's head upon a man's body!*

A violent shudder raced over Wentworth. With an effort, he forced himself to remain motionless. Then with his slow, steady hands, he picked up the bow, laid it aside with his violin and faced the creature. He bowed then, gravely, politely as a courtier.

"The god Anubis, I believe," he said softly. "How may I serve you?"

There was no mistaking the identity of the strange, glowing figure or its stiff archaic dress. It was that of the Egyptian god of darkness and death. Wentworth could not understand how he accepted that fact so calmly. Yet here he was, bowing....

The god was speaking now—harsh, grating sounds that came strangely from its jackal's mouth—the same language that once before Wentworth had heard upon the lips of Nephtasu. Only this time the meaning was clear:

"Guard us, O man, from these vermin who defile our name; who worship death obscenely and with evil, selfish intent. Thou art our protector, in the names of Isis and Osiris, in the name of...."

Voice and figure faded together into nothingness. A great calm was upon Wentworth and he went deliberately to his study, up the spiral stairway to his bed and sat down upon its edge.

Ram Singh came in the door. "Master, can I serve thee?"

Wentworth's head jerked. He looked down at his feet and found them bare. He saw dimly that his robe lay across the room from him. He reached out a quick hand, flashed on the light. He had no recollection of removing those garments and that fact puzzled him. He was very tired, but he had thought he still wore robe and slippers. Slowly, he stopped, picked up one of the felt slippers and put his hand into it. Wentworth started to his feet with a muffled shout. There was no warmth in his slipper. No warmth at all. And yet…?

"Ram Singh!" His voice was harsh in his own throat. "Ram Singh, hast thou—hast thou heard my violin this night?"

"When, *sahib?*"

"But now scarce ten minutes ago—in the music room."

Ram Singh's eyes were darkly puzzled. "I heard nothing, *sahib,* except thy breathing which seemed troubled, and once thou cried aloud a strange word which thy servant did not know."

Wentworth's breath came quickly, sharply. His mouth felt dry and he wet his lips with a tentative tongue. He almost whispered. "Was that word…*Anubis?*"

"*Han, sahib!* Yes, that was it!"

FOR A long moment, Wentworth sat upon his bedside and gazed searchingly into Ram Singh's face. The Hindu met his eyes proudly, sturdily. The light of dawn lay gray upon the window. With a harsh laugh, Wentworth thrust his feet into his cold felt slippers and instantly Ram Singh held his robe ready for his arms. With long strides then, the Hindu two paces behind, Wentworth hurried to the music room. Violin and bow lay as he remembered placing them two days before. The chin rest was cool and dry. He plucked up the instrument, began to play feverishly. Once more the haunting, measured notes of the melody he had thought he played before came distinctly, clearly, without faltering.

When it was finished, Wentworth turned again to Ram Singh, questioning him, but the answer was the same as before.

He had heard nothing save his master's troubled breathing. Wentworth nodded.

"My thanks, faithful one."

He went slowly back to his bed, but there was a new hope, a new lightness within him. His subconscious mind had transmuted that vaguely familiar phrase of the suicides' chant into a full score. And he knew now what it was—the hymn of Anubis, which the priests of ancient Egypt had chanted! At last he knew with what he had to contend. Those who, for reasons still unknown, had sent the scourge of suicide upon the country, had formed suicide cults under the guise of Anubis worship—or at least they chanted his hymn—Now if he could locate one of those secret cults, he would have a way of tracing back through its leader to the master-mind behind all this horror and death.

*His subconscious mind!* Wentworth smiled thinly. Well, Jamid Bey would put another interpretation upon what had happened. He would say that the ancients had sent him a message and a command… Dimly, Wentworth wondered where and when he had heard the hymn of Anubis….

WENTWORTH AWOKE four hours later with a sensation of blithe refreshment. Nita, hearing his voice over the phone, answered gaily with a brighter accent than Wentworth had known since the early days of their return voyage from Europe.

"But, Dick!" Nita cried. "When did you ever hear the hymn to Anubis?"

Wentworth laughed. "Darling, when you speak, it is a chant to beauty, and when you look at me…!"

The morning newspapers blotted out all his gaiety with their toll of new hundreds who had slain themselves. But they failed to repress his buoyant hope. He phoned to reporters he knew, told them about the song the suicides had chanted, offered to give them complete drafts of the music for publication and for comparison with what had been heard before the dynamite blast. He gave it as his opinion that all over the city, possibly forming in other cities, were cults dedicated to the worship of death....

"Now," Wentworth told Nita across a luncheon at Pierre's. "Now, perhaps they will think me dangerous enough to eliminate. If only they would attack me, I'd have a clue...."

Nita's white hand went to his. Her violet eyes, shadowed by the brim of a pert hat, were deep and tender.

"Dick dear, is there never to be an end?" she asked. "Never a surcease from this hourly risking of your life? These men are deadly. They use mysterious weapons of which no man ever heard before...."

Wentworth's gaze caressed her. "My sweet, if ever I commit suicide, it will be because your eyes no longer look on me as now...."

NITA LAUGHED with him tenderly. One of their stolen moments, so fleeting, so precious because of what might happen tomorrow, of what surely would happen some tomorrow to so valiant, so bold a champion. It was over even as it began, this moment of theirs. Nita's smile dimmed and Wentworth saw her arms tense with the clutching of hands in her lap.

"Ram Singh," she announced soberly, "is coming toward us."

Heads turned to watch the Hindu's proudly erect figure stalk across the dining room. Just the glimpse of him made all this crystal and tinkling gaiety seem trivial and effete. There was such strength and barren hardness about Ram Singh. He came from an ancient line of warriors and his service to Wentworth was the attachment of one brave man to another—such service as knights once gave their lords—rather than that of servant to master.

He halted beside Wentworth's table, raised his cupped hands to his turbaned forehead in salute, first to his master, then to the *missie sahib*, whom he admired and served with a devotion scarcely less fierce than that he gave his master.

"Has thy servant—" Ram Singh spoke in English for the benefit of the dozens of couples about them—"Has thy servant his lord's permission to speak?"

Wentworth nodded gravely, playing up to the Hindu's love of ostentation and brilliance. Ram Singh lapsed then into swift, harsh Hindu, his slightly nasal voice with difficulty concealing his excitement.

"*Sahib,* one came bringing a message to thy ear. A courier whose service it is to carry messages—" by which Ram Singh met a telegraph messenger boy—"brought a letter."

Wentworth asked a crisp question in Hindustani, then accepted the letter. Ram Singh folded his arms across his deep chest, staring coldly over the heads of the polite company. A joyous exclamation burst from Wentworth's lips, and he tossed the letter across to Nita.

"George Washington Bridge," he read. "The north footpath. At five this afternoon."

Nita's breath sucked in. "Oh, Dick, it is signed with—with the head of *Anubis!*"

Wentworth nodded gravely, the smile still on his lips, but his eyes darkened, hardening with determination.

"A tryst with Anubis!" he said slowly. "At last they consider me dangerous enough to eliminate!"

# CHAPTER 6
# TRYST WITH ANUBIS

ELEVEN MEN had died to throw the high-flung span of George Washington bridge across the Hudson. It arched from the heights on the New York shore to the Jersey Palisades like a thing more of air than of earth. Its giant towers and huge suspension cables all spidery from below; from its sprawling ramps with winding approach the roads which on the New York end coil off a half mile or more on each side.

None of the hurrying autoists, the bus loads of passengers pouring across in the thick of the afternoon rush-hour traffic paid any heed to the hunched-back man whose rubber-tipped cane helped him mount the slow gradient of the bridge's rise. If they did, it was with a little shudder of dislike, of dread. A creature so misshapen, so sinister of aspect, had no place amid the ethereal beauty, the slim grace of the bridge.

Richard Wentworth, strolling lightly across the northern footpath at a quarter of five, swinging a malacca cane in his gloved hand, looked at the hunch-back curiously. It was thus the Spider disguised himself when he went abroad at night in his own bleak, stern identity to deal out his stark justice. He wore just such a cape and black, felt hat....

Wentworth slowed his own pace a little, so that he kept behind the ambling cripple. Ceaselessly, but not obviously, Wentworth's eyes searched the passing crowds, the sleek stream-lined cars that droned past and the lumbering, bellowing buses. Was it from one of those that the attack upon himself would come? Or would some pedestrian like himself fire suddenly into his back? No doubt as to the purpose of the challenge. He had been dared to come here and tryst with Anubis and such a meeting

They meant his body to go tumbling with them to the water below!

68

could mean only death. The criminals would be prepared against his defense and his swift guns… Yet Wentworth strolled with a gay tune on his lips, cane jauntily swinging, for all the brittle readiness of body and mind.

So he came presently, fiercely alert, to the highest point of the bridge. He loitered there, stopped his whistling to gaze over the wide railing toward the waters far below. A graceful black speedboat was cutting back and forth in a wild demonstration of skill, whirling and skidding turns about invisible pylons, straightening out with a fan of white water from its sharp prow. The hunchback was watching, too.

Wentworth had taken such a position that the inner of the northern pair of thick cables—and the ties that bound them to the structure below—provided a shield between him and the passing cars. He glanced at the platinum-guarded dial of his watch. Five minutes of five. What, early to a tryst with the god of death? Wentworth's lips twisted, his raised brows mocking. His eyes remained dark and unchanged at his jest with death. He turned his back on the scene below, which was still engrossing the hunch-back.

Wentworth hooked his elbows over the top of the rail, tapping stick against his thigh with a dangling hand. The minutes crawled past, and despite his rock-steady nerves, he felt a tautening of all his body—a muscular readiness for action that must be coming now on winged feet. It lacked only a minute of the hour of his tryst. Surely Anubis would not be late?

AS THE seconds raced by, Wentworth's senses became even more acute. Nothing except an automobile could reach him in time now, it seemed. Near him was only the hunchback—who was beginning at last to amble on—and from the other direction, a pair of strolling lovers utterly oblivious of bridge or sky or crowd. But wait… Back there past the cripple came a solid block of men and girls in hiking costume, shorts and open-throated shirts, many of them carrying knapsacks on their shoulders. At their head, like an evil bird of ill omen, stalked a lean man with a prophet's ascetic, thin face. There was eagerness in his stride, an impetuous forward thrust to his gaunt, ungainly shoulders which jerked slightly with each step. He was bare-headed. A mane of thick, iron-gray hair swept back from a lumpish forehead, from beetling, strong brows.

Wentworth turned casually to face the man, his left arm swinging free, the collar of his coat gaping with his twisted, almost awkward posture. The cane lay across the fingers of his right hand as a man grips a sword-hilt lightly, firmly, but with a ready wrist. There was a smile upon Wentworth's lips—the smile with which he always welcomed battle or danger. Within him was a hard, blazing core of rage that burned the back of his throat and inflamed his brain.

Was this the man behind these mad, wholesale suicides? Was his the voice that urged men and women and youth of the land to death with the chant of dark Anubis on their tongues? If he was, then…! With scarcely a sideways glance, the man went striding past. Wentworth had a momentary impression of eyes that glowed from pits of shadows, of red, full lips that seemed strange in that ascetic face, of hands that were tapered and very white and had fine black hairs across their backs.

71

Behind the leader came the raggedly formed column, nearly thirty men and women in hiking garb. There was no laughter, no joy among them, nor any spring in their feet. But the weariness seemed rather of the spirit than of the body. Wentworth gazed at them, felt pity rise like a flood....

A deep, ringing shout came from the leader somewhere up ahead. The ranks halted. Their queer tiredness gave place abruptly to a feverish exaltation.... Far down the river, Wentworth saw a jet of steam spurt upward in a white plume above a factory and, seconds later, the hoarse wailing of a whistle announced that it was five o'clock. Even before the whine of the blast died, another sound came to mingle with it, to pierce and dominate its shriek.

The thirty hikers were singing, slow measured words in a weird minor key. Wentworth's cursing breath caught dryly in his throat. Hell itself had composed that music—

Above the voices boomed deep incantation of their leader in an antiphonic chant that blended with the others while it dominated them. And Wentworth, strangely, recognized that too—the exhortation of the priests! All this while, the white steam of the whistle blast still hung there, fading into air. Wentworth felt the strange, archaic music take hold on his senses and he wrenched himself from its spell, fire and ice in his heart. He flung sharp, taunting laughter to the skies, hurled himself with long, lunging strides toward the leader who, he suddenly realized, was goading these thirty to their death. Thought stopped him in his tracks. Good God! These thirty were planning to leap over the railing to their death in the waters below!

The leader was looking at him now, over the heads of the

suicide flock, eyes blazing, lips curved in mockery even as he chanted. His deep voice rolled on. Wentworth rasped a curse, charged again. A man sprang into his path from the ranks of the hikers, aiming a vicious blow. Wentworth paused in his plunge forward, his cane licked out in a rapier thrust and jabbed for the solar plexus. The man dropped, gasping, but instantly there were five—a dozen more—charging him, grasping for him with eager hands.

**WENTWORTH STRUCK** about him grimly with his cane, felled another man. His flying hands caught a girl's shoulder, hurled her against two who rushed to the battle. And all the while, they sang, chanted, as if they moved in the depths of unfathomable bliss in which nothing—neither pain, nor fear, nor death—could reach them. Behind, somewhere in the distance, the leader's deep voice roared. It was sharper, more excited, and it bred a fever in these automatons of death who struck viciously with open hands or tore with their nails and clawed fingers at the man who dared attack the thin-faced ascetic with the sensuous lips.

Wentworth realized suddenly that he was fighting to save these thirty lives as well as his own. He realized, too, how horribly he had been meant to die…! His guns were in his armpits and while he thrust violently with his cane, he snatched out one with his left hand, blasted lead upward over their heads. Not one man hesitated. Their exultation was too deep. They came hurtling in and one even threw himself deliberately high into the air as if hoping to stop the lethal lead with his body!

Over there, beyond the gap that separated paved roadway from walk, automobile horns were pouring a hell of noise toward the sky—a vast cacophony with a hundred voices, bleating, baying, rasping, trumpeting an excited protest to the skies. Wentworth felt a vast sense of unreality. It could not be possible that singing men and women were crowding him, jostling him steadily toward the rail, ready to hurl him and themselves from the bridge's awful height. Hands reached out to seize him, hands as slow and deliberate as the chanting dirge they mouthed. They were as inexorable as fate. Wentworth feared them suddenly, feared their steady, unwavering advance and the frenetic gleam in their glazed eyes. A shrewd trap they had set for him, cunning and terribly dangerous....

With a high, vaulting leap, Wentworth sprang to the rail, bracing an arm against the low-swinging cable that was between him and the death in the water below. His gun was ready and, deliberately, while hands tore at him, fought to thrust him from his purchase, he sought out the leader whose sonorous voice tolled him and these others to death. He raised his automatic and with the sureness that comes of long and painstaking practice and is born of necessity, he blasted lead at the priest of hell who urged them on.

The leader did not move, but a woman sprang high into the path of the bullet and fell with a shattered skull. A second shot found its lodging in the breast of a boy who leaped eagerly to the sacrifice. And the priest kept up his chant, and on all sides, the haunting, terrible strains of the hymn of the dead continued.

Two men had hold of one of Wentworth's legs now, trying to drag him from the cable. He swung savagely at their heads with the flat of his gun, knocked down one, two—and others leaped eagerly to take their places.

Wentworth was fighting grimly now, with hard-curved lips and eyes that flashed with lightnings of anger. Life was fierce and strong within him as was his hatred of that demon leader. But each blow he struck at these half-demented pitiful who singing, rushed in to kill him, was a pain in his heart. His rage was all concentrated on one man now and it was thrice as bitter because of the deaths of those two poor wretches who had leaped into the path of his lead. There could be no more of that shooting.

His cane was wrenched from his hand, mightily whirled, smashed down on his left arm, which alone saved him from being hurled off into space. Crushing agony, then a cold numbness gripped it. It still clung, but the grasp was feeble. If help did not come soon....

WENTWORTH'S VOICE leaped from his throat in a great, ringing shout. From fifty feet away, it was answered, the harsh rage of the reply slashing through the chant. Wentworth could not look that way, but he heard one man's chant end in a shriek. He hurled himself violently from the railing into the thick of the fight, striking savagely with his fists—with the useless automatic he still grasped. The men charged straight toward him. Nothing except the physical impact of the gun, sufficient to hurl them from their feet, could stop them. No pain, no mere blow of the fist, could stay their mad death march. Nothing but death itself....

Those who had fallen and were unable to continue the fight, crawled toward the railing and climbing painfully, hurled themselves to the death that awaited them in the waters below. Wentworth caught one, tried to tear him back, but the man fought like a fiend, striking, kicking and plunging downward finally with the chant of death still whipping from his lips. A woman helped a faltering man and, together, arms locked about each other; they sprang out into the abyss of destruction.

Wentworth had a space to breathe finally and looking through the tangled battle ranks he saw the hunchback striking mightily with his cane, knocking men and women from his path indiscriminately. From somewhere among the automobiles, a woman's shrill cry rose:

"Oh, God above! Look, look! *It's the Spider!*"

So indeed did the creature seem who battled through the thinning ranks to Wentworth's assistance, black cape flying from his shoulders, black hat upon his head and a sharp, strong-nosed face that was as sinister as the man's deeds.

But now there came another rush of ten, twelve men together. One or two fell before Wentworth's driving blows, a third, a fourth, but the others bored in, overwhelmed his striking fists. They did not attempt to harm him, but seized arms and legs and, chanting more vigorously, more triumphantly than ever, moved toward the railing. Wentworth's mind reeled. They meant to— *to throw him off!* They meant his body to go tumbling, whirling downward to be smashed to pieces upon the surface of the water, which would be as hard as concrete from any such height as this. The chant rose about him, strenuous, jubilant.

One of the men who held his kicking feet straddled the rail, poised there, waiting. His voice was sweet and clear, lovely as a dream. The second man was over the rail now, and a third… In a moment—in another little, pitiful moment—they would leap and carry him with them to his death!

But good heavens, this couldn't be! He, the Spider, must survive. He did not think of personal life, though it was strong and vibrant within him. Nor did he think of Nita, with her white, soft arms and deep, violet eyes. He thought of the fearful thing which the priest of hell would accomplish—of the thousands and tens of thousands that man would toll to death with the bell-like exhorting of his deep, sonorous voice. It must not be allowed!

More men than the Spider knew of this infamy, but only the Spider *believed!* He must live to carry this warning to humanity. He must strike once more, win through for the sake of mankind. With these thoughts, a new vigor sped through his muscles. With a mighty thrust of his legs, he freed one foot, though in accomplishing it, he sent a chanting man tumbling and spinning to his doom far below. In the next instant, the robed hunchback struck terribly at the group with his clubbed cane.

Two more men were wrenched loose, but a third locked both hands about Wentworth's left arm. Then, with a high, triumphant cry, he hurled himself bodily from the railing, sure that his mighty death grip would drag down the Spider, too!

## CHAPTER 7
## BATTLE ON HIGH

**W**ENTWORTH HAD only a half-second's warning of the man's intention to drag him down from the bridge. The mere idea would have frozen most men into an immobility that would have meant death, but for the Spider, that much time was enough. It gave him an instant to brace a foot on the base of the balustrade, to close his right arm more snuggly about the rail and to tighten the muscles of his left arm against the shock that the other's plunging weight would cause.

Fortunately, the man was slightly built and under middle height. Otherwise, even with warning and preparation, he must have yanked Wentworth loose from his precarious perch outside the bridge rail. As it was, the shock shook loose his foothold, numbed his already injured left arm and nearly tore the grip of his right hand loose from the railing. Clinging, with teeth locked, face grim with strain, Wentworth turned his bitter eyes toward the rest of the men he had fought to save. There were only a few left, four on their feet battling the robed cripple who fought gigantically with his heavy cane....

His was no thrust technique as was Wentworth's, but a heavy battering that smashed through an arm guard and smacked at the heads beneath. But there was no help there for Wentworth.

The battler would have no chance to turn and haul him to safety. A shuddering jar rippled over Wentworth's body and he felt his right hand, nails digging into the concrete, slip a half inch. The man, dangling on his arm, had jerked at him in an effort to pull loose his hold. He repeated the action and Wentworth lost an entire inch. Good God! A few more like that and he and the suicide would pull him whirling down to death!

Wentworth's muscles were cramping with strain and there was a strength-draining fatigue throughout his body. Even his superb strength could not much longer resist the drag of so great a weight. Wentworth jerked his head. He must not die yet. The Spider had work to do, a duty to perform. For this man clinging to him who was so avid to die, there was no hate, only pity in Wentworth's breast. But the fellow was dragging down thousands of his fellow beings with him if, struggling and yanking so, he succeeded in killing the Spider!

A frantic jerk cost Wentworth another inch. Three more lost and he would be gone. He must act quickly then. Two of his defender's assailants were down, but the other two were pressing hard and a third was crawling along the pavement to flank him. No help there!

With a curse of despair, Wentworth jerked up a foot, let drive at the face of the man who sought to murder him. The panted chant that still gasped from those lips stopped. There was a final desperate pull that almost cost Wentworth's life; then the fellow let go and went whirling, whirling down—and down—and down....

Wentworth watched with helpless fascination, saw the tiny spinning doll-thing that was a man smack against the water, throwing a great column of spray toward the sky. Feebly, then, Wentworth lifted a foot to try for a renewed purchase on the balustrade, but he had slipped down too far; his strength was too far spent. He no longer could look over the balustrade. He could not tell whether the robed man was triumphant or had fallen, too, as prey to the mad band. He only knew that the feeling was fast leaving his right arm and that his left was too badly strained to be of any help. He could not lift it as high as his shoulder....

Then his fight had been vain! He had saved no one from this lunatic plunge to death. The leader had gone away—Wentworth realized that for long minutes he had not heard the great, soaring voice of the man. But what did any of these things matter? Within seconds, his hand would lose its last hold. With the thought, his frantic nails slipped another lost inch along the railing. He fought the paralysis in his left arm, almost afraid to move lest he lose what purchase he had. He had no confidence that his left arm would be of any help, even if it topped the balustrade, but it might enable him in some way to regain a grip with his right.

FIERCELY, INCH by inch, in a struggle that brought the beads of pain-sweat to his forehead, he forced that almost paralyzed left arm upward. The stab in his shoulder-joint, muscles straining over a distorted joint, was almost unendurable. A little hoarse cry gasped from his lips. Then, crazily, the twisted arm slid over the balustrade.

Even as he succeeded, a sharp, triumphant cry rang out and a second later, the strong-nosed face of the caped man peered over at him. Hand linked to arm, a foot against the balustrade, a long heave, and they stood side by side surveying the scene of the battle. Two men lay upon the pavement. The two others had disappeared, gone overside unseen while Wentworth fought for his life.

"Thanks, great one!" Wentworth panted.

"*Wah!*" said the other, harshly. "Thy servant is a feeble old woman! For three minutes, those four jackals kept me in play!"

Wentworth flung a quick look about. While the battle raged, men had stood back. Now they came from all directions, hopping across on the supports between roadway and pavement. A police whistle keened somewhere down the bridge, and on each side of the pair, men packed the walk.

One sound predominated among all the gabble of noise and voices; the sibilant whisper: "Spider!" ran like quick-silver through the throng.

"We were somewhat unfortunate, Ram Singh, in our choice of disguise for you," Wentworth murmured, gaining control over his breathing. "Did you see where the leader went?"

"*Wah!* He was a coward!" Ram Singh spat on the pavement. "He fled I know not whither at the first sound of battle. Nor did he leap overboard."

So that trail was lost almost on the instant of discovery! Wentworth was suddenly aware of the temper of the crowd. One man, red-faced and shouting, stood beside his automobile shaking fists at the sky.

"The Spider killed them and threw them in the river!" he yelled. "The Spider killed them! Threw them in the river!"

Wentworth looked at the man with narrowed eyes and remembered that somewhere in the battle he had dropped an automatic. He glanced about and did not find it. A frown twisted his forehead. That gun was registered in his name. If it were found, he would have no chance of escaping some sort of police charges in connection with this battle, especially since the Spider apparently was supporting him. But there were other worries. The red-faced one might succeed in stirring up a mob to furious anger and he and the Hindu too were trapped here against the balustrade.

However, Wentworth still had another holstered automatic. He looked at the red-faced man whose bellowed charges were being repeated until others took up the cry. Man had seen, but few had been able to understand what was happening. Certainly, they had seen the tall, broad-shouldered one kick into perdition several men who were holding him. The yells grew into a great, sullen roar, a sound as of waves crashing upon dry rocks. No mistaking that moan of hate. They had seen fellow men done to death, and the Spider was a man with huge prices on his head for murder… *Kill the Spider!*… Only one thing held them back—the fear of this fierce slayer of men… *Kill the Spider!*… If they were to rush him now, altogether, certainly he would be able to shoot many. Let the red-faced man lead. He surged forward as if he heard the unbidden call of the mob he had raised… *"Kill! Kill! Kill the Spider!"*

**WENTWORTH SNAPPED** an order at Ram Singh and together, in one graceful leap, they gained the broad, round cable that arched upward toward the towers at each end. In a single kick, they were rid of their shoes and, with deliberate sure-footedness, one behind the other, the two men began to mount the great suspension conduit. For fully thirty seconds—time for them to take a dozen paces upward—the amazement of the crowd held them motionless. Then their anger burst like a wave against a cliff, hurling menacingly cries of rage upward. A hail of wrenches and tools that had been snatched from cars followed. One man yanked out a revolver—it was the red-faced one— and suddenly Wentworth realized why the fellow's face had seemed familiar. It was Red Almaro, a man equally good with a gun or a bottle of "soup," a safe-cracker who was employed most frequently by—Wentworth's automatic slid to his hand and blazed once—by Seltzer, a planner of crimes! The man was an agitator he chose to use on occasion to excite mobs. The recoil of the weapon skillfully taken up in his arm. Wentworth holstered his weapon again. Red Almaro was wringing a bullet-smashed forearm; his gun had gone into the river.

Wentworth, with Ram Singh behind him, was beyond the reach of casual missiles now, fifty feet along the cable had carried them high above the heads of the howling mob below. On one side, the killing mob; on the other, the sheer abyss of death. The wind was stronger here, tugging at clothing, and Wentworth could hear the dull snapping of Ram Singh's cape, threatening to hurl him overboard. And the Hindu needed his arms for balance, could not use them to hold the cloak close against the thrust of the wind.

"Truly, master," Ram Singh gasped, "you are all seeing and most wise. Fortunate indeed for thy servant that thou gavest orders for my socks and thine to be thoroughly rosined!"

Wentworth smiled grimly. There was an agony in his left arm, and the wind was a constant peril. Furthermore, another score of feet ahead, the cable began to mount much more steeply, an impossible climb. The mob was below them, unarmed, apparently, until the police came.

"This is the best chance we'll get, Ram Singh," Wentworth said shortly. "Straddle the cable and grip one of the rods that lead downward with thy feet. Then give me the hump off thy back."

He suited his own action to the words and, seated, twisted about to receive the "hump"—a long, thick package that had been strapped to Ram Singh's back. Quickly, Wentworth tore the wrappings from the bundle, took out the two articles it contained.

"I anticipated the possible necessity of such an escape," Wentworth explained. "This is not a full-sized parachute, but with water below us, it should be sufficient. That black launch there is the *Nita*. Jackson will pick us up a few moments after we strike the water. The best plan will be to yank the rip cord now, let pilot 'chute float loose and then jump."

He yanked the ring, twisted about and watched the tiny pilot 'chute jerk and tug clear of the bridge in the freshening wind. He smiled at Ram Singh and both clambered to their feet. The river was far and flat below them; Jackson's boat a tiny, darting, black bug.

"Ready, my warrior?"

*"Han, sahib!"* Shall thy servant leap first?"

"Together, Ram Singh!"

"Together, *sahib!*"

The shout of the thousands below them echoed upward in a

vast hollow moan as they realized that their prey were prepared to leap. They recognized, too, the packs upon their backs.

A police officer's whistle blasted. "Halt! Halt! Or I'll shoot!"

"On the count of three, my warrior," Wentworth said calmly. "One... two... *three!*"

# CHAPTER 8
# AMBUSH FOR THE SPIDER!

IN THE cabin of the launch which Jackson was speeding down the river, Wentworth stripped awkwardly, permitted Ram Singh's swift, expert taping of his injured arm. Strained ligaments were tautly braced and the swollen shoulder-joint proved to be only badly wrenched.

"It's a wonder you weren't broken in half by that idiot," Jackson growled from the hatchway. "If I'd had my Springfield."

"With the wind variations, you'd probably have shot off my other arm," Wentworth said, but his smile took the sting from his words. "I think we can expect Police Commissioner Flynn to be waiting for us at the apartment. I lost one of my automatics."

The greetings of Wentworth's butler, Jenkyns, when he returned home, confirmed his prediction. "Commissioner Flynn is waiting, Master Dick," he said, voice smooth and without stress despite the worry in his old, blue eyes.

Wentworth strode energetically into the drawing-room with a smile and a hearty greeting for the bony commissioner. "Hello, Flynn! You certainly traced that automatic quickly."

Flynn's face was sour. His narrow, long head, with its wiry hair, was held stiffly, but there was a frosty sparkle in his eyes.

"Fool stunt, Wentworth!" he grumbled. "Jumping off bridge. Suicide bug get you?"

Wentworth fumbled a cigarette from his case, offered Flynn one, then dropped down on a lounge with careful consideration for his left arm. Jenkyns was at his elbow with a lighter and Wentworth nodded to him. "Refreshments, Jenkyns, and have the coffee for my *café royale* very cold."

Jenkyns withdrew with: "Very good, sir!" Wentworth welled smoke out of his mouth, settled more deeply into the cushions.

"I'll tell you all I know about the business and then you can ask questions," he said. He gave the details of the reception of the note and the battle on the bridge. But he told it all without close attention, for his mind dwelled on other things, turned somberly to his failure on the bridge and complete failure to get a clue. He still had no lead to the man who used the seal of Anubis—the chief of the Suicide League—and, damn it, the thing would grow rather than diminish. Thousands died today, tomorrow they would perish by tens of thousands.

Flynn grunted as his account ended, asked acidly: "Don't suppose you and the Spider exchanged cards?"

"Scarcely necessary, my dear fellow." Wentworth waved his cigarette airily. "We know each other by sight. Never introduced at the best clubs, of course. He said, however, that the Suicide League had run him to earth, also sent him the same challenge I received."

Flynn grunted, took a sharp, long-legged turn up and down

the room. "Have to keep your gun for a while. Inquest, dead man, dead woman."

Wentworth nodded. "The leader was urging the men to kill me and themselves. Naturally I tried to wing him. Those two jumped in front of my bullets."

"Why not kill Almaro?" Flynn spat out. "Rat. Must die some day. Shot at you. Justifiable."

WENTWORTH GRINNED. "I never needlessly kill a fellow man," he said, but his eyes were veiled and secretive. Red Almaro undoubtedly had been planted on the bridge to lead mob action if the suicide automatons failed in their attack. That meant that Almaro—probably Seltzer also—was involved with the ascetic leader.

Wentworth was glad now that his bullets had not struck down the chanting leader. It had been the madness of battle, the effort to save the thirty men and women from death, that had inspired the shots. With the man alive, there was at once a greater and less chance of the Spider's ultimate triumph. Greater because the leader offered one more chance of finding the moving forces behind the Suicide League. Less because his survival meant that now the full strength of the criminal alliance would be turned toward accomplishing the Spider's death.

Flynn broke in on his thoughts. "Governor Kirkpatrick," he grunted. "Be here tonight about ten. Wants to confer. His home."

Wentworth's face brightened. "Splendid!" he cried. "I haven't seen Kirk since—" he made a wry face—"since he refused to pardon me on that trumped-up murder charge that afterward was quashed."

Flynn nodded sharply, took the drink Jenkyns offered, tossed it off neat. "Something like that will get you some day. Better lay off amateur detecting."

"How would you solve the crimes if I did?" Wentworth jibed amiably.

Flynn shook with an internal laughter that scarcely stirred his lips. "I'm no detective," he admitted, "but morale is good. More men qualifying every day as expert marksmen. Promote them if they're good. Break them if they're lousy."

"You're efficient," Wentworth admitted, "but the police organization is intended to fight only the ordinary criminal. Give them a man who operates in a different routine, or such a group as the Suicide League, and they're up against it."

Flynn grinned, his thin, firm lips hard against his teeth. "That's why I'll be sorry to see you burn. No bother about stuff on bridge. Just show up in the morning."

Wentworth nodded as Flynn rose to go. He appreciated that the commissioner had not attempted to wrest information from him about the Spider, understanding the *noblesse oblige* between him and the apparent Spider on the bridge. Flynn knew, without the attempt, that Wentworth would not talk.

At the door, Flynn turned. "This suicide business—what causes it?"

Wentworth frowned. "I think it's a drug or a gas administered some way, possibly a virus of some disease, though it acts more like one of the former. No way of telling yet."

Flynn nodded. "Hope you're right. Can stop that. Mass hysteria, more difficult. Phone description of that preacher to head-quarters, will you? Don't know the questions myself."

Wentworth bowed assent. He liked the new commissioner, a retired major-general, who had taken the post after Stanley Kirkpatrick, the Spider's enemy, but Wentworth's friend, had been elected governor of the state. There had been years when Kirkpatrick and the Spider had fought each other bitterly and with a deadly skill; when Kirkpatrick had suspected his friend, Wentworth. But finally both perceived they fought for the same cause and a truce had been formed—a truce in which Kirkpatrick agreed to help the work until such time as positive proof of the Spider's identity should fall into his hands. Then he would forget friendship, and prosecute to the utmost of his ability.

ONCE, WHEN Wentworth had been framed for murder on what seemed conclusive evidence, Kirkpatrick had resolutely refused a pardon, and... But that was water under the bridge. Wentworth knew that he, too, would have made the same decision, as often he was called upon to do in his battles against the Underworld; decisions sometimes between loved ones and the fate of the city at the hands of some mad, murderous genius of crime. Even against Nita....

Jenkyns interrupted his thoughts by entering with a portable telephone. "The call you have been expecting, sir," he said. "Mr. Jamid Bey."

Wentworth took the telephone eagerly and the rich, oddly accented voice of the Egyptian came to his ear.

"I see by the newspapers," said Jamid Bey, "that Wentworth

*sahib* did not tell the newspapers everything about Anubis and his hymn."

Wentworth asked lazily, "And what did I omit, Bey Pasha?"

The Egyptian laughed softly. "You did not tell them that you *dreamed* the music or that Anubis appeared to you!"

Wentworth was silent to that, eyes narrowed and thoughtful. Now how the devil did the man know?…

Jamid Bey's laughter was still in his voice. "I have received my answer, and it is permitted that I tell you… certain things. Will you do me the honor of a visit this evening? Say, about eight?"

Wentworth, still lazily, said, "Certainly and with pleasure. You're a damnably mysterious fellow, Jamid Bey. The Carlston, I believe?"

Ram Singh renewed the bandages on Wentworth's arm as he dressed for the evening. The soreness was increasing, but with the help of the taping, he could use it with some stiffness and pain. There was a sharp excitement in Wentworth's breast. He had told no one, save Nita, that the music had come to him in a dream. He remembered what he thought at the time—that the Egyptian would consider it was a message and a command from the ancients. He moved impatiently as Ram Singh carefully bandaged him.

Finally, the last meticulous details of his dress were completed, Jenkyns advanced to adjust the customary cornflower in his lapel, to set the white, satin-lined Inverness cape about his shoulders, to hand him silk hat and gloves and gold-headed cane. The old man's ruddy face was worried. Wentworth pointed the cane at his chest.

"You have not been sleeping, Jenkyns. If you wait up for me tonight, I shall certainly fire you." He looked affectionately at the man who had served his father before him. He felt an abrupt, painful wave of longing for the hard, lean man he remembered from his teens—the man who, one tragic day, had died with his wife in an Alpine accident.

"Tell me, Jenkyns." Wentworth hesitated, the longing within him an ache in his throat. "Tell me, do you think my father would have... approved of his son?"

Jenkyns looked down quickly, lest brimming eyes spoil his perfect composure. "I'm sure, Master Dick, that he would."

"Even... the Spider?"

Jenkyns' eyes lifted, became firm and direct. "Your father was a brave and a just man, Master Dick—far beyond his time. He would have grieved for your lost happiness, sir..." Jenkyns hesitated and Wentworth knew what he thought—knew because of the smile that lighted the old man's face whenever Miss Nita came to the apartment. Jenkyns, too, longed for the day when the long, black cloak and the Spider's seal would be laid aside forever.

"But he would have honored you," Jenkyns finished, "and I do and all of us do, Master Dick, for a brave and upright man."

**WENTWORTH HID** his emotion with a light laugh. "You'll probably have a chance to tell that to a judge some day, Jenkyns."

He sauntered out, but the nostalgia of the moment, the thought of Nita, remained with him as Jackson wheeled his new Daimler town car to the curb and opened the door with military precision. Wentworth's eyes took in the dark street in one swift glance, caught no hostile move.

"I'm a little ahead of time, Jackson," Wentworth said. "You might go once about the park."

The Carlston Hotel was a quietly elegant hostelry in the East Sixties, its facade no more conspicuous than that of the wealthy residences about. A butler attended at the locked, outer door; the lobby was a formal reception room and registration was in the client's own suite. There were no mere "rooms" here—Jamid Bey's elevator was his exclusively. Jamid Bey's own *fellaheen* salaamed Wentworth into his suite with much less insolence than before.

The same remarkable transformation that had been wrought on the ship was apparent here, too. The two white-robed *fellaheen* escorted him with sidling, almost backward footsteps, as if he had been royalty, along a richly carpeted hallway to a room where Jamid Bey, in native dress, rose formally to greet him. In the midst of oriental splendor, a fountain splashed and tinkled sweetly. The ceiling was domed in blue, dappled with winking golden stars, and twisted fluted columns supported the arches that marched about its sides.

Jamid Bey himself wore baggy silken trousers and tunic of purest white over which a long, flowing coat, sea-green, with macabre embroidery in gold, made a gorgeous contrast. Only now were Wentworth's hat and cloak, gloves and cane, taken from him and he sank down upon floor cushions as gracefully as his host. His shoes seemed awkward beside the crimson morocco slippers on Jamid Bey's feet.

The Egyptian's dark face was lean and stern. Wentworth's own countenance resumed grim lines now that the formality of greeting was over. Wentworth could not forget that he walked with death and that this man had once ordered slaves to kill him—if he gave a certain signal… They chatted casually until coffee had been served and long-tubed water pipes offered. Then Jamid Bey lifted his handsome dark eyes to Wentworth's face.

"I have been answered," he said gravely. "It is permitted that I tell a little of what is known in the hope that your splendid strength will assist us to punish evil-doers and retrieve our secrets."

Wentworth nodded, eyes keenly alive on those of his host. "And the information about the visitation by Anubis?"

"Mere thought-wave susceptibility," he said, then paused, giving the impression of choosing his words carefully. And once more, as on the occasion when the two sword slaves had killed themselves at the command of this extraordinary man, Wentworth had a feeling that the Egyptian had difficulty in phrasing his thoughts in English—as if he were translating from some strange tongue. His accent was more pronounced now.

"Secrets of the priests of Isis and Serapis, Ammon and Aphrodite, of the Pharaohs of ancient days, were held by certain leagues called mysteries. They were never common knowledge, never the property of the Alexandria library that was destroyed. They knew a drug that can make a man howl like a dog and become a dog, too, in his habit and his living. And there is a certain secret temple light—but these things are not yet for the world. The Wise Ones keep them…."

WENTWORTH DID not lose his attitude of eager listening, but his mind was racing. He knew that those things were whispered, of course. They were a part of the beliefs of man, like the prophesy of the second coming of the Messiah, and the immortality of the soul. Men talked of the old wisdom and tried to look knowingly. It was true that ancient Egypt had built a practical steam engine on Pharos lighthouse at Alexandria… With a mental shrug, Wentworth listened. True or not, it was obvious that Jamid Bey believed….

"Among the drugs in the custody of these ancients was a chemical once given to traitors that they ought destroy themselves," the Egyptian said. "A renegade priest only recently stole the secret, but when he… paid, the formula was no longer in his possession. That drug came to America aboard the *Plutonic*, but who now has the custody or why it was employed aboard the ship, I do not know."

Jamid Bey ceased speaking and bowed his head as if in prayer. Wentworth frowned at his water pipe, thoughtfully drew its cool, fragrant smoke into his lungs. Rubbish, many men would call this, and ignore it as such. Wentworth's own skepticism was aroused, but the fact remained that men and women *had* slain themselves in a mad saturnalia of death aboard the ship. Furthermore, the lexicons of modern pharmacy revealed no such drug. Chemistry knew no gas or liquid or freakish compound that could cause such behavior. There were certain germs that drove men mad, or even caused self-injury, but this passion for death by any and every means, regardless of pain… Wentworth had seen many strange things in his travels of the world and he had fought many curious and loathsome devices of death....

Jamid Bey frowned. "You do not believe," he said, "and for that I cannot blame you, nor shall I strive to convince you. But I am permitted to tell you this much more; the drug is a purplish powder, tasteless and soluble in any liquid that is not strongly acrid. It is called *melakheen* and came first from the Hindu-Kush, as it is now called."

Wentworth said carelessly. "It is permitted to know just which of the fellow passengers of the *Plutonic* had contact with this renegade priest?"

Jamid Bey laughed harshly. "None of them! Not one has even been to the town in which this priest... paid!"

Wentworth felt a grim smile tug at his mouth corners at Jamid Bey's hesitancy concerning the punishment of the renegade priest.

"And how," Wentworth asked, "did this priest... pay?"

Jamid Bey's mouth was grim and a strangely mocking light touched his dark eyes. "The priest, my friend, committed suicide!"

It was a few moments later that Nephtasu, as at some given signal, entered the chamber. Two of the white-clad *fellaheen* stole across the room, drew aside great brilliant carpets, stood in half salaam until she had passed, then stood against the entrance with folded arms.

Wentworth rose to greet her, aware as always of the fire that lurked in her long green eyes. Her dress of plain, heavy black silk, would have been undistinguished upon any lesser person. But draped exquisitely to the lithe contours of her body, it was superb. She had built the bright flame of her hair into a coronet of long braids, wound again and again about the small, tight shapeliness of her skull. At her appearance, Jamid Bey seemed to draw into himself. For a half-hour, the talk wound aimlessly through Egypt and the Mediterranean and dwelt at length upon the tragedy of the *Plutonic*....

Wentworth's mind was heavy with thought at his departure. He leaned back at ease while Jackson sent the Daimler swiftly toward the Governor's uptown home, depending on the doughty ex-sergeant to guard against his enemies. He was a little early, and he was pleased at the prospect of seeing his friend, the governor, alone. He eased his arm against the cushions, closed his eyes. A queer man, the Jamid Bey, and altogether mysterious. There was something utterly inexplicable about his abilities as a hypnotist, about his feat of knowing precisely the details of this visit of Anubis. Might it be possible that some post-hypnotic…? But the Spider's was not a will that yielded to another's, even though that other was Jamid Bey....

HE REVIEWED the story he had been told and was of two minds whether to accept the story or not. Of course, he had no choice but to repeat it. He must not risk the possibility that, strange as it seemed, Jamid Bey told the truth. Even if the drug, *melakheen* actually were to blame, there was still the difficulty of finding how it was distributed.

Wentworth opened his eyes, glanced sharply about. They were rolling swiftly up Fifth Avenue in the Seventies, a lonely stretch beside the park. If his enemies sought him out now… Abruptly, he jerked forward on his seat, a warning cry in his throat... but it was unnecessary. Jackson had already slammed on the car's powerful brakes. Tires squealed on the pavement and Wentworth sat, helplessly gripping the robe rod on the back of the front seat while the heavy town car bore down on a young girl in its path.

The girl had acted with such unexpected quickness that had made it impossible to avoid her, leaping from the pavement to a position squarely in front of the Daimler. She stood there now, her head flung back and her young throat swelling with a song that came to Wentworth even through the squeal of swiftly applied brakes. He cursed. Already that song was drenched in blood, stained with the death of thousands... the dread hymn of Anubis!

The heavy Daimler slid to a halt within inches of the girl. Wentworth tore his eyes from the would-be suicide, flung a swift searching look about him. No suspicious car lounged alongside, no gun blazed from a darkened doorway. But his mouth was thin-lipped as he thrust open the door and in long strides reached the girl's side. A policeman hurried across the pavement, took one glance at the impeccable evening attire and began to growl at the girl....

"Not at all, officer," Wentworth interrupted. "With your permission I am going to send this young lady to a hospital in my car. If she is left to herself...."

The officer stepped back with an awkward salute and Wentworth spoke rapidly to Jackson. He handed the unresisting girl into the back of the Daimler and it whirled away.... A glance at the street sign showed he was only a block and a half from the governor's town-house. He pushed on afoot, frowning heavily. Just another of the would-be suicides that thronged the city....

He was still alive to the possibility of attack and he had hoped to foil assassins by the unexpected placing of the girl in his car. It might be that he had decided unwisely.... His mind returned to the problem of the supposed suicide drug. Food supplies, or tobacco might be used for distribution. They had been employed for vindictive purposes before this. Possibly....

Wentworth became aware of the man in the shadows a split-second before the man intended. His action was as swift and keen as the eyes that had detected the lurking menace. Wentworth dropped to one knee with the speedy coordination of brain and muscle that made him the formidable warrior he was. In the same motion, his gold-headed cane flashed out. The unexpected thrust hammered the man in the shadows back against the stone wall that sheltered him. Then the fellow ducked aside from the cane's point, charged forward wildly with a long-bladed knife held low against the hip!

## CHAPTER 9
## CRYSTALS OF DOOM!

WENTWORTH HAD a single glimpse of the knife-man's dark, passion-knotted face as he pushed in. The surprise of the sight almost cost him his life. Unless he had gone mad, the man with the knife was... But it couldn't be! It was impossible that this lurking assassin was *Jamid Bey!* For one amazed instant, Wentworth remained motionless and the knife flashed surely, strongly for his throat. Only by a prodigious effort, by the exertion of his utmost will, did he throw off the daze of his surprise and shrink aside from the blow.

The blade whistled over his shoulder, and the man stumbled, lost his balance for a moment. Wentworth sprang away from the threat; his two hands closed on cane and handle. With a wrench and a harsh whisper, a sword flashed in the dim rays of the distant street light. Blade in hand, Wentworth did not wait for the dark knifeman to renew the attack. He sprang forward with the sword flickering to the kill.

Only for an instant did the man stand crouched. Then he whipped the knife through the air in a frenzied, vicious throw. In the same moment, he twisted about in flight. Wentworth did two things with lightning-like rapidity. His sword swerved to meet the flying blade, sent it ringing futilely to the pavement. Instantly then, he dropped the sword and its cane scabbard and flashed his right hand to an automatic. The gun leaped to his hands, ready and eager, but... the assassin had vanished!

A moment before, he had been darting straight toward the building across the street, as if he sought refuge in the entry-way that opened there; the next, he was swallowed up in nothingness! Wentworth raced toward the spot where last he had seen the fleeing man, and checked, staring grimly down at the roadway. The disappearance was explained. A man-hole cover had been removed from a sewer opening and into that, feet first, the flee-ing Egyptian had jumped.

Wentworth's breath had quickened and he could feel the fierce, hot pumping of his blood. Memory of that snarling face in the darkness was a crazy whirling pinwheel within his brain. Cautiously, he stepped back from the spot of black emptiness in the middle of the street. It was all queer and twisted. In the first place, he did not believe that Jamid Bey would have stopped to commit an assassination himself. Why should he, when he had a dozen eager slaves to do the work for him? That one factor alone seemed to preclude the possibility of what he believed he had seen. His eyes were playing him tricks… yet the Spider was not given to such mistakes!

Whatever he had seen, the assassin had now escaped. Those sewers ran on for miles beneath the city streets. There was no way of divining the assailant's route. Frowning, Wentworth returned his gun to its holster, stooped to pick up his sword cane and join it together again. Then he caught up the savage knife which had nearly taken his life. It had a long, leaf-shaped blade, pointed and fuller near the tip than at the hilt and it was made not of steel but of cleverly wrought bronze. Wentworth balanced the thing on his palm, hurried on to the governor's house.

THE TWO police officers on constant guard there stared at the knife curiously. The wooden-faced butler offered tentatively to relieve him of it, but received a curt refusal. Still holding it carelessly in his left hand, Wentworth sauntered into the reception room, and a few moments later, the governor entered with his characteristic swift, firm stride.

"Dick, damn your soul!" he cried. "I didn't go to Albany to forget you, you know, or… What the devil have you got in your hand?"

Wentworth took the knife in his right hand—his left arm was

throbbing with the exertion to which he had forced it—held the blade out, hilt-first.

"That knife almost prevented my coming here," he said with a quizzical smile, "So I just brought it along as a souvenir."

Kirkpatrick shot a sharp glance from his blue eyes, weighed the weapon on his hand. "A nice toy. And the lad who played with it?"

"Got away."

Kirkpatrick sniffed. "Incredible! I've seen you shoot."

The two men stood in the midst of the formal reception room, smiling slightly into each other's eyes—tall, straight men with the lean jaw of those who do things, and the balanced poise of those who know how they should be done. Kirkpatrick would have been the taller but for the slight droop in his otherwise military bearing—the weight of his official cares, he said—and he was older by ten years. Gray was powdering his temples, though his pointed mustache was coal-black and vigorously pointed. His dress and toilet were meticulous, a gardenia graced his lapel, but there was nothing foppish in his appearance. He was too vital, too strong-faced. Saturnine lines creased his cheeks and the bones of his cheeks stood out boldly. He smiled a little, laid the knife gently down on a mahogany table.

"Up to your neck in trouble, as usual, Dick," he said quizzically. "Was the gentleman who attacked you Eastern, as well as his blade?"

"Egyptian," Wentworth said shortly, frowning, drew out cigarettes and lighter. The two men smoked in silence a few moments, eyeing each other with the warmth of friends who have battled against and for one another. Kirkpatrick, who had once refused to pardon him on a murder charge; Wentworth, who had once been on the point of killing his friend to save a city. And each had approved of what the other did.

"I'm making fair progress cleaning out the grafters," Kirkpatrick said presently, "but the warfare lacks the zest of our former battles."

Wentworth's lips twisted. "I thought the Underworld was clean of weeds, but there's a fresh and formidable crop." He laughed harshly. "Damn it, Kirk, I feel old... old! I can't make a dent in this problem of suicides."

"I thought you and—" Kirkpatrick's eyes twinkled—"your friend, the Spider, did right well on the bridge."

Wentworth shrugged. "We didn't save a single man. We were lucky to come out of it alive. If it hadn't been for the Spider...."

Kirkpatrick's eyes grew merrier. "It was very fortuitous that he carried *two* parachutes in his hump, Dick!"

"It was," Wentworth admitted cautiously.

"Strange, don't you think?"

"Still barking up the old tree, eh, Kirk?" Wentworth countered. "Still accusing me of being the Spider?"

Kirkpatrick said, "Oh, no, no! You misunderstand me, Dick." They both laughed and the governor poured drinks, offered a glass to Wentworth. "An old toast: 'Success to the Spider!'"

POLICE COMMISSIONER FLYNN and his staff soon arrived; chairs were drawn up, and the conference got under way. Wentworth still hesitated to tell what Jamid Bey had related, doubting the truth, wanting proof before he spoke. He listened to full reports on the suicide census. Seven thousand to date in New York, with Chicago reporting a swiftly mounting tide that indicated the plague had taken a terrible hold there, too. A half-dozen scattered industrial towns reported the terror of their populace and a death list that waxed more and more formidable.

Sneed Jenkins, dubbing himself Ambassador of Good Cheer, was flying about the country, instigating amusement programs that apparently accomplished nothing at all. Reading the digested findings, Wentworth saw a name that tautened his muscles. In two or three of the reports, the name of Lars Jorgensen, Captain, retired, appeared as present, but surviving suicide disasters. Wentworth caught up a fountain pen from the long, green-baize table the counselors circled and made a black line beneath each repetition of the name. Kirkpatrick watched with shrewd eyes and nodded as he read the clippings.

"A suspicious circumstance," he agreed, "and coupled with the fact that all those deaths occurred on his ship, most damning. Yet our investigation shows nothing suspicious in his activities. He seems morbidly fascinated by the suicides, according to men who talked with him. He is eager to tell anyone who will listen about the tragic affair on the *Plutonic.*"

"Sneed Jenkins?" Wentworth queried.

Kirkpatrick smiled, and one or two others of the consultants laughed a little. Flynn leaned his long, bony arms on the table, clasped the thin hands. "Ridiculous little runt," he said. "Does no good, but might. Certainly no harm." Heads nodded so unanimously that Wentworth's eyes narrowed.

"I'm suspicious of everyone," he admitted, "even of myself sometimes. Remember that old motto: *'Beware him of whom everyone speaks good.'* I don't want to croak at the feast—"

Kirkpatrick shrugged, tossed a sheaf of papers across the table. Detectives had been watching Jenkins, too, and found nothing evil to report. He never eluded them and the surveillance continued day and night.

"And then," said Kirkpatrick in his clipped, metallic voice, eyes intently on Wentworth, "there is Jamid Bey, an Egyptian, as is the signature on the challenge sent Wentworth. He keeps very much to himself, but his men come and go at will. You see, gentlemen—" he turned to the others about the table—"while most of you were unwilling to concede that there was merely a human, criminal agency behind these deaths, it has been my experience that when both my friend, Wentworth, and the Spider agree about a thing, it is usually pretty close to the truth. I admit, however, that the investigations I ordered have revealed nothing conclusive against anyone even remotely connected with the deaths."

A butler was passing unobtrusively behind the seated men, renewing the contents of their pitchers of iced water. Wentworth signaled him and requested that the juice of two lemons be brought to him separately. His eyes were sharp and contradicted the lazy ease with which he had relaxed into his chair. No one paid him any special heed. Kirkpatrick was still talking, outlining the necessity for prompt effective action, looking to

Commissioner Flynn, then to the youngish, broad-faced man named Christopher, who represented the Secret Service and who, Wentworth recalled, had been aboard the *Plutonic* also. Finally a small glass-full of lemon juice was produced and Wentworth poured himself a carafe of water, then deliberately allowed the lemon juice to spill slowly into it.

KIRKPATRICK'S EYES swept toward him and paused there, his speech broken off. Wentworth scarcely noticed, so intent was he. Gradually, other talking died and all eyes concentrated on the steady, lean hands about the careful business of pouring. Half of the lemon juice was exhausted and still he dripped the yellow liquid tediously, drops at a time.

Christopher's face was amused, though his eyes remained keenly alert. "A new drink, Mr. Wentworth, or a conjuring trick?"

Wentworth let his lips smile, but didn't answer, as he continued the slow manipulations. A sudden suspicion had recurred to him as to the means by which the suicide drug was spread among the populace. Food and tobaccos were difficult of access, but the city water... Well, at least he could make the test Jamid Bey suggested. Abruptly he ceased pouring the lemon acid into the glass, eyeing it with mounting excitement. Good God! Was it possible Jamid Bey had told him the truth after all? It seemed... Carefully he allowed one more drop to plop into the water. Wentworth, watching, felt his breath clog in his throat, felt the dry-mouthed suspense of unbelief. Tiny beads of sweat popped out on his upper lip, on his forehead.

Flynn growled, "What the hell is that?"

"A conjuring trick," Christopher insisted good-naturedly.

Wentworth touched his tongue to his lips, drove himself from his bewildered engrossment with an effort, lifted his eyes to Kirkpatrick.

"City water?" he asked hoarsely.

Kirkpatrick nodded and asked no question, but the eyes of the two men were keenly locked. Wentworth got slowly to his feet, a sense of discovery racing all through his body like the blood-flood of a great joy.

"Gentlemen," he said heavily, forcing the words to calmness. "Tonight an Egyptian friend told me that he remembered vaguely a drug known as *melakheen* which was reputed to drive men to suicidal death. He said that this drug was soluble except in acidous water, when it precipitated in purplish crystals. Gentlemen, you all saw me drop acid into this water and now..." He held up the glass. Iridescent against the light, *the water was full of slowly settling purple crystals!*

Flynn cried fiercely, *"The suicide drug!"*

Christopher remained silent with an inane, startled grin on his face and Kirkpatrick's jaws set so that the muscles knotted along the bone.

"Yes, gentlemen," said Wentworth, his voice jubilant now, "and unless the governor has a member of the Suicide League in his employ, it means we have found the means by which the city is being decimated, the suicide drug is in our city water-supply!"

# CHAPTER 10
# THE SPIDER IS READY!

WENTWORTH'S STATEMENT drew out gasps of startled disbelief, cries of incredulous joy from the counselors.

Christopher said heatedly: "I don't know of any suicide drug. And besides, to impregnate the water like that, tons would have to be dumped into the reservoirs. It would have to be impervious to filtration and alum treatment."

"This drug is *melakheen* and it's capable of all of that," Wentworth explained sharply. "As to tons of it, the crystals generate other crystals, instantly soluble except in acid; tasteless even then. I think Governor, that we better acidify the water system of the city."

*"Melakheen?"* Christopher repeated, *"Melakheen?"*

"Organic," Wentworth told him. "An indigenous plant of the Hindu-Kush, akin, I understand, to our own *loco weed*. I just learned of its existence today and the idea of testing the city water only came to me while we sat here. I advise, Kirk, that the findings here not be made public, or the Suicide League is apt to find another means of distributing the stuff."

Flynn was cursing thinly under his breath. "I drank the damned stuff. Drink quarts a day."

"The strong willed rarely suffer from it," Wentworth said dryly. "And in this case, the alcoholics would be exempt, too." He said these things in a light, mocking tone, but bitter rage was in his heart. If only he could have known this days ago, back on the ship, he might have prevented all those deaths and the subsequent ones ashore. Jamid Bey had known of the drug and probably guessed how it was distributed since he knew the details of the chemical's behavior. Kirkpatrick was talking, his crisp voice ringing with confidence....

"All other cities must be notified at once," he said. "It is possible that the secret will leak out, but now that we know the acid test, it need not concern us particularly." Even Kirkpatrick was jubilant, joking a little in a serious proclamation.

Wentworth shook his head. He did not share in Kirkpatrick's confidence, though he agreed that the warning must be widespread. Men clever enough to have instigated the plague of death without detection—without, to date, any slightest hint of their identities—could devise a new means of distribution.

"Kirk, will you do me a favor?" he requested lazily. "Publish this thing, broadcast it, since it is bound to leak out anyway; and give me full credit for the discovery?"

Kirkpatrick frowned a little, but he knew his friend too well to think that the request was dictated by personal vanity as it was clear, from various facial expressions, that others did.

"The credit is yours," the governor said, his saturnine face still somewhat puzzled. "I see no reason to deny it, and I suppose, as you say, that it is just as well to broadcast the information."

Wentworth smiled slowly. "Thanks a lot," he said. "Would you mind if I excused myself now? I have work that must be done." Governor Kirkpatrick's nod was quite prompt, but his smile was quizzical. "Look out for the Spider," he advised gravely, "or he might beat you to the kill."

"He usually does," Wentworth agreed suavely, "but somehow I feel that this time, the triumph will be mine!"

Wentworth donned his cape impatiently, caught hat, gloves and cane from the butler and went rapidly down the steps of the governor's house. He found he had left the captured knife behind and sent the butler after it while he waited, restlessly eyeing the shadows. He had a special reason for retaining the weapon. Not that he thought Jamid Bey, under any circumstances, would show any facial expression he might wish to hide....

JACKSON ALREADY had the Daimler before the entrance, standing ramrod-straight beside the closed door. Finally the butler returned holding the knife gingerly. Wentworth nodded his thanks, went rapidly down the steps. He had not previously had opportunity to consider the details of the attack upon himself, but it seemed to him that the latter half, the knife-throwing, was impromptu.

A prickling of cold touched the back of his neck. The plots of men he could and often did foil—though the men struck like a snake in the dark—but if he had found the asp this time, it would have been by the purest luck—only because of his long years of habitual caution.... He was inclined to think that, in the darkness of his car, he would not have found the reptile—until the venom first found him!

His hand was steady as he lighted a cigarette and there was a twitching, thin smile upon his lips. The enemy had shown himself able, very able. Perhaps, the Spider....

Jackson was speaking again, without movement of his lips. "Miss Nita, sir, is in the car with another lady…."

Wentworth finished lighting the cigarette, handed the knife to Jackson. His mind seized eagerly on the information. Another lady?—That he did not understand. But if Nita had come for him… He sprang into the tonneau as Jackson opened the door. In the darkness, his hand found Nita's as the car slid forward.

"Something has happened, darling?"

Nita's hand pressed him. "Denver Dane has joined a suicide cult headed by a man named Jackson Grant, who must, from the description, be the same man you met on the bridge. Helen Stuyvesant has come to take us to their midnight meeting place. It is already quite late…."

Helen's voice came brokenly through the darkness. "Oh please, Mr. Wentworth. Please! If you can only save Denvie….!"

Wentworth frowned, reassuring her automatically. But it was not of saving the boy that he thought most, though naturally he would do what he could in that respect. Despite a widespread search, the Priest of Anubis—as Wentworth had come to call the man in his own mind—the Priest contrived to carry on his evil work and to assemble a new band of recruits whom the suicide drug would destroy. Cold anger tightened into a frown. The man must be stopped!

But first Wentworth must milk him dry of all information. There would be no better time than tonight….

"How are you dressed?" he asked in the sharp, muted voice that Nita knew indicated his deep thought.

"Sport clothing," she answered quickly. "Gaudy and not very neat."

"Excellent! I'm going to signal a taxi for you girls. Jackson will follow you, then signal with three blasts on the horn to stop...."

The change was quickly made and Wentworth rapidly drew the shades of the tonneau, touched a button beneath the edge of the cushions. The entire left half of the seat slid forward smoothly, revolving as it moved, revealing a wardrobe and a tray which, when folded upward, became a shelf on which make-up materials were fixed by small, tight, elastic bands. A mirror was in a panel, ringed with brilliant lights. Wentworth went swiftly to work.

Beneath his practiced fingers, the lean tanness of his cheeks became sallow; the skin tautened over the cheekbones; the sensitive lips became hard and straight. A beaked, powerful nose was built over his own. Now, bushy black eyebrows, a wig of lank hair....

For a moment, Wentworth inspected the result from every possible angle. Then he smiled, slowly, with the sinister lipless mouth he had created.

Tonight, the Spider sought his prey. He reached out a swift hand and darkness filled the car again....

# CHAPTER 11
## THE WINE OF ANUBIS

WHEN WENTWORTH descended from his car a little later, it was neither as the suave, elegant Richard Wentworth who had entered, nor as the Spider, with his hunched, be-caped back. He wore—as jauntily as any youth of Hell's Kitchen—a suit that fitted him too tightly, with padded, exaggerated shoulders. The hat, set too far back, too much to one side on his head, was a much-cleaned white felt.

In the darkness of the street, he passed easily for what he seemed. But if anyone had glimpsed his face… No one did, however, and he sauntered, swagger-shouldered, beside the two girls toward the meeting place of Jackson Grant's suicide cult. They three talked loudly, brazenly, while secretly exchanging details in hushed voices that had no carrying power at all. Then, on a street corner, they parted—Nita and Helen to stroll on, Wentworth to circle a few blocks and return later. Even before he was ready, the hirelings of the Suicide League might learn his identity and it would be well for the two not to be identified with him in the public eye.

Twenty minutes later, Wentworth presented himself at a tenement doorway, open to the night, where the meetings were being held. He walked in with his swaggering shoulders. In the darkness, a hand touched, then held his arm.

"What the hell?" Wentworth gasped in his best tough accent, fists balling.

"Whither goest thou?" a voice, sepulchral and deep in the darkness, asked him.

Wentworth fidgeted. "Cheez, why didn't you say so? Ain't no sense in all this here…."

"Whither goest thou?" the voice persisted.

"To consort wit' dem what would worship Anoobis," Wentworth gave the pass phrase.

"Ah! And then, my friend?"

"Cheez, dis is wors' than dem Masons!" Wentworth still fidgeted against the hand. "To feast an'… and mayhap to die."

"The third floor," said the voice, "and think not that, mocking, thou mayst come, for Anubis will surely see thy heart."

"Cheez!" Wentworth gulped, and made his hurried way upward. There was a hot burning in his brain. So they snared their prey with mumbo-jumbo ritual, made it difficult and exclusive to enter apparently. Once in the halls of Anubis, they would be fed the drug in great quantities. The end was the chanting automatons of the bridge… Damnable, this was, but what in the name of heaven was its purpose? Those who died were indiscriminately selected. What profit was there in wholesale murder without purpose or direction?

But there *was* a motive, no doubt of that, no matter how deeply hidden, how much obscured by meaningless gestures… Wentworth's eyes were hard and glittering. Perhaps the Spider would learn tonight—if he were not detected by the killers. At a door behind which a deep rolling voice spoke urgently, Wentworth was stopped again. "The word, friend?"

"Aw, nerts! Anoobis is lord of death and of eternal happiness."

"Enter, friend! And may the eternal happiness of Anubis be yours."

"T'anks," said Wentworth, with mockery deep in his soul. "T'anks, pal."

THE VOICE within was still for a moment and Wentworth

114

He lifted the jar and hurled
it into the priest's face!

slipped in through the door, stood motionless with keen eyes secretly darting about the jammed room within. The walls were elaborately painted with crude representations of Egyptian figures, stiffly postured in obscene poses. No seat was visible, but fully fifty persons sprawled or crouched upon the floor. Over the whole, a garish blue light waxed and waned, its source at first difficult to discern. Lest he attract attention to himself, Wentworth crouched down on his heels against the wall, hat on the floor beside him while he studied the full details of the room.

He saw now that the light seeped over the tops of the walls and he understood then that these paintings were on some removable substance, braced canvas probably. Even knowing that, Wentworth felt keenly the oppression, the emotion of the room. It was close with the quick, hot breathing of the crowd. A pervasive, heavy scent originated in a tripod toward which everyone faced. Wentworth had picked the probable exits now. He turned his attention to the central figure of all this multitude, Jackson Grant.

A single glance showed that this was indeed the man of the ascetic face—the one, who, on the bridge, had exhorted more than a score of enthusiasts to their deaths.

Now he wore gowns that truly made him a priest of hell, as Wentworth had dubbed him. He stood before a great squatting statue of Anubis of the jackal face. Obscene liberties had been taken with the god's identity and person... But Wentworth had no time for the idol, probably papier-mâché. He focused on the priest as did all others in the room.

The Priest stood behind the tripod, draped in great long robes, his head covered by an Egyptian head-dress with the imperial cobra-sun symbol upon his forehead. As he gestured, wielding the mighty weapon of his rich voice, his robes showed scarlet in the glow of the tripod from which heavy coils of incense smoke whirled upward; then ghostly blue in the cold radiance of the pulsing lights.

"The sacred wine!" Grant cried portentously. "The blood of sacrifices to Anubis! Come forward and drink of joy, and glory, and great happiness! He signaled with sweeping arms and, low and distant as the chanting of priests in the great sun-temple of Thebes, came the wailing, first notes of the hymn to Ra. Wentworth's eyes narrowed and he nodded. A powerful phonograph hidden somewhere. All very cleverly staged, and yet, though he knew this, he could feel the grip of emotion about him, the surge of wild exultation. A girl sprang to her feet with a low, intense cry and, moving as in a trance, stole toward the tripod where the high priest of Anubis stood, moving his arms in a sweeping incantation that merged with the chanting—louder, more dominant now.

The girl went on her knees before the tripod and caught up a great bronze ewer that stood beside it, lifted the thing eagerly to her lips. When she had drunk, she turned toward the others, lifting her arms as did the priest and a powerful start pulled at Wentworth's heart. It was Helen Stuyvesant! Her black, tight hair was haloed by the red glow of the tripod; her face held a queer, drunken exultation; wild enthusiasm.

"Anubis!" cried her throaty voice. *"Anubis!"*

As if she were a magnet, others, men mingled with the

women, rose to their feet. A few voices muttered in rhythm to the chant. The sound deepened and grew as others and still others joined, moving toward the ewer that Jackson Grant called the wine of Anubis—*wine of death!* Wentworth choked down his wrath. He was not here to kill—yet. He was here to see to what ends this Grant would go—to learn, if possible, how all this horror was motivated… His spirit writhed within him as he rose to join the procession to the ewer. These fifty went to their death as surely as if that Egyptian jar from which they drank contained poison instead of the eating ferment of the suicide drug. He kept his face turned as he neared Helen Stuyvesant. In her present maddened state she might betray him!

ONCE MORE, warily, Wentworth's eyes swung about the room. He noticed then that there were four men at equal distances about the walls who did not join in the general procession, but who stood with lowering gaze fixed on those who filed past. They were chanting, adding their volume to the others, but on their faces was no inspired emotion. They were guards, beyond doubt part of the organization.

Amid the turmoil about the altar, Wentworth caught a glimpse of Nita's searching face. She made an excellent pretense but Wentworth knew her eyes sought him. He could make no signal. Much better if she did not know his whereabouts. How long would the mummery proceed, Wentworth wondered. How many times did they drink of the drugged wine before Jackson Grant began his exhortations to death?

In front of him, a man moved stiffly, with jerking muscles, pulled at his head as he approached an extreme of hysteria.

Beside him, a woman laughed softly and throatily to herself. Her face was vacant of all thought, all intelligence.

The devil! These already had drunk before! It must be so, for the prodding voice of Jackson Grant, the vast choir of chanting that must come from a radio-phonograph device, were not enough to have stirred them so soon. Wentworth threw a quick glance at his watch. It was nearly two o'clock in the morning.

Wentworth was nearing the ewer now, nearing his turn to drink from the jar of death. Slowly his jaw set, his eyes flickered over the four who stood guard. Could he convince these fifty of the chicanery going on here? Could he save them from the death toward which the voice of the priest of hell drove them like a gigantic, irresistible whip? Wentworth choked down mocking laughter. Since when had the Spider weighed chances of success? He must make the attempt, though it meant battling not only the guards and the priest, but probably the very persons he fought to save!

Calmly, Wentworth made his plans. His hands touched the twin automatics in his armpit holsters. The white hat was in his hand, and with swift fingers, he punched the crown inside out. The underside of the brim remained white, but it had become the slouch, broad-brimmed headgear of the Spider. He tugged tentatively at the hem of his coat, felt the shoulder seams give a little, nodded. A jerk and the garment would part at the shoulders and fall from him. The reason for those heavily padded shoulders would become obvious, for the black long cape that was the Spider's well-known garb would flutter out like a battle flag!

The man with jerking muscles stepped forward and dropped on his knees to drink from the ewer again. He lifted it eagerly, gulping, spilling a wet tracery of wine on his face and clothing. Wentworth stepped forward and, reluctantly, the man yielded. Wentworth did not kneel. He stood straight, lifted the jar, abruptly reversed it and hurled it directly into Jackson Grant's face.

The priest went backward and down under the blow of the ewer. Wentworth jerked free his cape, dragged on his slouch hat and faced the stunned worshippers from behind the tripod, its red glow brushing a shadow over his sinister face.

The four guards against the wall had been taken completely by surprise. Now, as they reached for their guns, the Spider's automatics slid into his palms.

"Drop those guns!" he shouted. *"I am the Spider!"*

One guard reeled against the wall. In the absolute silence that followed, the clatter of his falling weapon was a great sound. Somewhere behind the scenes the chanting died into a mechanical scratching that told of an untended phonograph. It signified a new source of danger for Wentworth—the person who had left it. The Spider's icy, menacing eyes swept the company. Then both of his guns crashed; the sound billowed against the walls and stunned men's senses. Two of the guards, furtive guns still only half-exposed as they sought to kill from the shadows, were dying on their feet. One stood starkly, head driven back by lead through the canvas of the painted walls. The grip of it sustained his weight for long seconds, while the death blood trickled from the hole the Spider's bullet had bored in his forehead.

THE OTHER man thumped to his knees, swayed a moment there, and, with a gasped-out curse, smacked his face down on the floor. The guard who had dropped his gun bolted for the doorway. His dash spread panic through the crowd.

"Halt!" Wentworth shouted harshly. The man turned, cowering, hands abjectly raised. The fourth guard seized that moment to try what his mates had failed to do. He got his revolver out and half-lifted before the Spider's gun crashed once more. The guard spun backward, whirling, against a woman. His hands caught at her as he went down, ripped her clothing. Her scream mingled with his dying cry.

"I'll kill the next man that moves," Wentworth said coldly. *"The Spider swears it!* Do you need to be told more?"

Only then came sounds from the crowd, an exhaled hoarse sigh that seemed to be the single breath of all that packed the room. Wentworth looked the men and women over slowly while the smoke of the incense rose about his shadow-painted face.

"This man I have knocked down—this high priest whom you worship—is a fake!" Wentworth declared vehemently. "He lures you here with fair talk and promises of happiness. Fools! *The happiness he brings you is death!"*

Wentworth's ears were keenly attuned, listening intently. At precisely five minutes after two, Jackson would phone the police a tip-off as to the location of this meeting, if the shots had not already caused an alarm. Wentworth guessed that they had not.

"The sacrificial wine that you drink," he explained heavily, "is filled with the suicide drug—the drug that has made so many people kill themselves. Did you know that Jackson Grant led the men and women who jumped from the Hudson River bridge? That was the fate intended for you…!"

Somewhere behind the false waits the chanting started again, and the Spider listened grimly, tried to drown it out with his powerful voice. He singled out the man whom he had completely terrorized with lead.

"Bring me the dead!" he ordered sharply. He had to fire twice more with his guns before the man obeyed. Then slowly, fearfully, the dead men were dragged to where Wentworth stood behind the tripod. The crowd was engrossed now, watching things done that penetrated even their drug-laden consciousness.

Deliberately, Wentworth stooped beside each of the three dead men, pressing the base of his cigarette lighter to each forehead. Where he touched, a scarlet spot sprang into being, a symbol of sprawling hairy legs and venomous fangs, *the seal of the Spider!* So Wentworth marked those whom, in his stern execution of justice, he slew. The sight of his brand rocked the crowd like a cold wind that broke through the chanting of the priests. WENTWORTH SAW Nita gliding toward the sound of the phonograph, a competent, small automatic grasped in her hand. Joy surged in him. If she could stop that infernal chanting… Minutes had flown. Even now, Jackson was phoning his message to police. Soon the radio cars….

Nita had disappeared, but the chanting continued and the crowded men and women before him had been left too long free of the Spider's dominant voice. They were swaying to the rhythm of the chant, and the mutter of their voices was beginning to rise. Suddenly a challenge boomed forth from Jackson Grant.

122

"Kill! Kill! Kill!" he cried. "Kill the traitor! Kill the defiler of Anubis!"

Wentworth whirled with a jerk of guns, but Jackson Grant no longer lay where he had fallen. He had been shamming unconsciousness at the end then, to catch Wentworth off guard. And now he had taken refuge behind those canvas walls, where he could lash his hounds on to the kill without being seen himself....

Other voices picked up the chant: "Kill the traitor, kill the defiler of Anubis!" It rose with the same weird, wailing cadence of the hymn.

It was obvious to Wentworth now that the stuff they had drunk made them extraordinarily sensitive to suggestion—suggestion and rhythm. Perhaps, he could counter that... Behind the canvas, a woman screamed sharply and the cry was cut off. He heard the light crack of Nita's automatic; then the rising chant swallowed the sound.

Too late now to check this rising fury of destruction. The police would be here within moments. For once the Spider might turn to the assistance of his beloved.... In a long leap, Wentworth reached the canvas wall, smashed his fist through its fabric, and yanked savagely. The screen tottered, wavered and, as Wentworth leaped clear, a section that covered half the length of a wall toppled straight forward upon the heads of the chanting men and women.

The boom of Jackson Grant's voice cut short and from the black mouth of a hallway, gun-flame lanced at Wentworth. His gun blasted a fiery answer, but he fired high. He did not want

Jackson Grant to die just yet. He snatched out a pocket flashlight, hurled its meager beam down the hallway. A hoarse shout tore itself from his throat. He lunged forward, cursing, his gun a hot, hungry thing in his hand.

Fortunate indeed that he had fired high, though even now it might be too late to make any difference. Dimly, as through a veil, he could see Nita down the hallway, directly in the path of his fire. She had been hanged to the ceiling....

## CHAPTER 12
## THE SPIDER FALLS

A S WENTWORTH, eyes tightening with fury, raced down the hallway, he heard screams and shouts break out behind him. He heard a door crash before an assault which he knew could be only the raiding police. But there was room in his mind for only the one thing—the necessity of reaching Nita before... before....

NITA VAN SLOAN

A terrific blow smote his outreaching gun, doubled it back on his wrist as if he had plunged headlong against a solid wall. His gun made a sharp thud. Yet before him the way seemed clear.

Even while bewilderment mocked him, Wentworth's superbly trained reflexes were at work. With a violent effort, while his heart cried aloud for him to dash on and save Nita, he fought to check his forward lunge, jerked back his head and twisted it aside. Quick as he was, he could not keep himself from pitching headlong against the barrier that his gun had slammed against.

His chest struck heavily; his head, thanks to his sharp effort, touched only lightly, but he reeled back with the wind driven from him, frantic with effort, almost stunned by the impact… against an invisible wall! He saw then what had happened. He had run full-tilt into a door of glass dropped across the hallway, a barrier that had not cracked, nor yielded to his violent charge.

And just beyond it, Nita swung with a rope biting into the white flesh of her throat, strangling while she fought desperately to ease the strain upon the halter that was killing her. Her eyes were already glazed, too despairing to see; her lips parted with the out-thrust of her swelling tongue. But even in her agony, Wentworth fancied her lips moved, thought she called his name.

A sudden thought was a blast of pain in its clarity. That shot at him! It had been fired from just this spot, but whether before or after the glass was lowered, he did not know. Wentworth jerked up his head. He knew where he had aimed, knew that his aim rarely failed. There, near the ceiling and squarely in the center of the glass panel was the round, crystallized mark of his bullet! He frowned, whipping his agonized mind from the thought of Nita. Then, if the screen had been already dropped when the shot was fired…!

With frantic fingers, heedless of the shout and pound of the police behind him and the death they would bring to him— heedless of everything save Nita's rescue—Wentworth fumbled with the center of the bullet-proof screen of glass. Somewhere here there must be an opening, for it was from the center of the hall that the shot had come… Something clicked beneath his stumbling fingers; his breath gusted out in a sound between curse and prayer, and suddenly his hand shot through the glass, a narrow panel swung wide. Not a wide opening, just room for a hand with a gun….

That was what Wentworth thrust through the port, a hand and a gun. No need now to think. Only one thing was possible. He must cut that strangling rope with a bullet! He could not aim, for he must point his automatic sharply upward. Nita had almost ceased to struggle. This first shot must be the last.

The hand of a lesser man might have trembled, but Wentworth's was as steady as on the pistol range, though his face was a distorted mask of twisted fury and despair. Now! *Now!*

The automatic bucked in Wentworth's hand, slamming it sideways against the glass, almost fracturing his wrist, numbing it with pain. It was almost torn from his fingers. Hurriedly, agony biting at his soul, Wentworth withdrew the weapon, eyes on Nita's darkening face, striving frantically to get his left hand, which still could shoot, through the gunport. Dear God, why didn't Nita fall? The bullet had hit the rope. He knew it had.

There was a muffled snap, and all at once, Nita was on the floor. She fell heavily, laxly, lay in a contorted attitude with her legs doubled under her, the cheap finery of her disguise awry…. WENTWORTH JERKED his hand clear of the opening and, holstering his gun, he fought the panel of glass, jerking, pushing, seeking its lock.

Wentworth had forgotten that he wore the damning robes of the Spider, that three men back there in that den of battle bore his mocking seal upon their foreheads; he had forgotten that the police were here, hot upon his heels by this time, that the lives of thousands of his countrymen depended upon him.

Another disastrous thing Wentworth forgot… In the temple was one man, not under the influence of the drug, who had seen his companions fall beneath the wrath of the Spider's bullets. He could tell the police that down this hall, the Spider had fled following a woman's scream!

But Wentworth only battled against the stubborn panel that simply would not yield. A barrier he could not pass and on whose other side lay the woman he loved, unconscious, perhaps dying, for lack of the help that his arms could give….

Suddenly, sharply, a cry ran down the corridor where he battled, a cry that had heralded a thousand attempts upon his life, whose driving savagery he had fled through all the years, less in fear than in the necessity of surviving that he might help those who hunted him.

"*The Spider!*" a man shouted. "There's the Spider! Oh, God…!"

Wentworth whirled, gun leaping to his hand. But even as his trigger finger contracted, he jerked up the muzzle. The Spider did not fire on police, not even to save his own life. His gun flash was an instant ahead of that of the uniformed man silhouetted against the pulsing blue white lights of the temple of Anubis. If Wentworth had allowed the bullet to speed true, the man would have been hurled lifeless back from the doorway. But the Spider shot high, and the police man—

Wentworth's shoulders struck back hard against the glass barrier. He knew an instant of commingled pain, self-mockery and despair. For a long moment he stood, spread-eagled against the bulletproof panel. Deliberately, shouting incoherent words, the policeman fired again.

The Spider crumpled forward on his face....

NITA RECOVERED consciousness with a tight, hard pain in her throat and a buzzing in her head, deafening one instant, receding the next, to allow bursts of words to beat upon her throbbing ears.

"I tell you I killed him!" a man swore hoarsely above her. "I killed the Spider. I hit him once, beat him to the shot and jammed him back against that damned glass wall; then I hit him again and he flopped forward on his face. You can see the blood there. See? A lot of it. A man who bleeds like that...!"

Not all of that at once, but in little snatches, for the policeman was repeating himself a great many times in his loud boastfulness. And Nita, felt vaguely that what was being said should be important to her... and realized he was talking about Richard Wentworth, her Dick....

The cry that rose in her throat made only a faint moaning. It went unnoticed by the men about her. When she moved, it was unimportant, too, and Nita's trembling hands went to her throat and found there the remnants of a rope. Then, flashingly, memory came back to her. She had seen Dick had been fighting against that wall of glass.

Nita was on her feet before the policemen whirled toward her, looking a little startled, as if some one quite dead had stood up to confront them. Her face was smeared with the exaggerated makeup she had used; her clothing was cheap and tawdry, but even so, these men should have seen the dignity and the strength that was there; should have seen scorn in the curl of her lips.

Nita looked at the policeman who was saying again that he had killed the Spider, and suddenly, she was laughing. It sounded hoarsely and it hurt her throat, but she laughed. The man was young and boastful and this night he hadn't shaved, so that the short blonde hair bristled on his cheeks and caught little yellow gleams from the many flashlights. He had a stubborn jaw, but his eyes were without intelligence.

"I beat him to the shot," he was saying stubbornly once more.

Nita's laughter broke. "You beat the Spider to the shot? *You?* Why you poor fool…!" Her voice was coarse and unnatural. "You fool! The Spider never shoots at police."

Nita's hands were not at her throat now, but clenched fists shaking in the face of the men who stared at her. "Fools! All of you, fools! Damn you, damn you…!" Her voice went dead in her throat. She cared nothing for them. It was Dick, her Dick. She swayed and dropped down on her knees. There was an irregular dark splotch on the dusty floor and, hesitantly, Nita's hand went to it. If Dick was dead, where was he?

"Dick?" she breathed. She stayed there like that, with her hand in the blood that these men said meant a mortal wound—meant Dick, her Dick, was dead….

Slowly Nita lifted her hand, stared at the stained fingers. She moved them slowly, drew them closer to her white, twisted face….

"Good God, *miss, you can't…!*"

"She's crazy!"

The sergeant bent forward. "Listen here," he said roughly, "don't do that! You must be crazy. No civilized woman...!"

He reeled back with the red stains of Nita's fingers across his face. She was on her feet again, but she was no longer laughing. Her face was taut and fierce. She turned and ran, stumbling down the hall. She had to run. Sobs were thrusting up through her throat now, tearing as if each one were a hard, hot ball of steel....

Nita never knew where she walked that night, did not even know when men jeered at her. But once when a taxi driver stepped into her path, she lifted her face... The man reeled back, babbling. His voice rose behind her. "Damn! Damn!" he cried. "Damn! Damn! She has blood all over her mouth...!"

NITA'S LIPS twisted. Dick's blood, his sweet, dear blood. She wanted its stain there always on his lips to remind her... She stopped abruptly, looking about her, and found the shadow under the elevated railway structure growing gray with dawn.

Finally, somehow, she got to her apartment. Her Great Dane, Apollo, whom Wentworth had given her and trained, started to prance, his great, heavy body vibrant in welcome. But Nita ignored him and he stopped and looked up into her face and whined low in his throat.

Nita told herself over and over again that Dick could not be dead. Suddenly she remembered something. Those policemen had been disputing whether the Spider actually had been shot. That meant, it meant...! Nita jerked to her feet. Somehow, Dick had got away, wounded though he was. But all that blood....

Nita's heart fought against her reason, which said no man

wounded like that could live to walk at all. Then her heart gave a great bound. Jackson…!

Frantically, Nita snatched at the telephone. Jenkyns had heard no word. Ram Singh? He had gone out soon after Master Dick. Oh, then the two of them had Dick in their care. It *must* be so. No god could be so cruel as to destroy… Nita's face seemed wasted as she looked at it in the mirror of her bath. Her hand rose hesitantly to her lips. Suddenly, vigorously, she began to undress, to bathe. Morbidity was foolish. Soon Ram Singh or Jackson would phone her… Memory kept nagging at her brain: "… a man who has lost that much blood…!"

All that day, Nita sat bolt upright beside her phone, waiting. Her maid moved on tiptoe through the apartment, carrying away the dishes Nita could not touch. Late in the afternoon, Nita called for the twentieth time to hear Jenkyns say, huskily: "No, Miss Nita, no word at all. Why… why don't you come over here, Miss?"

Nita went. Well on toward morning, sitting in the chair that Dick always preferred in his den, she sagged finally into exhausted sleep. She was there when Ram Singh entered quietly, stood before her, his dark face harsh and drawn. She awakened and sat looking at him. Then, slowly, she got to her feet, caught up her coat. She had not removed her hat. A great joy and a great grief struggled within her.

"Take me to him," she ordered.

THE BULLET wounds were in shoulder and lung. One transfusion already had been performed when Nita arrived. Wentworth lay motionless, white and drained, upon a narrow bed. His doctor rose, thin-lipped, coarse red beard disarrayed head weary.

"You gave him a transfusion once?" he said.

Nita nodded, removing her coat, rolling up her left sleeve. Her violet eyes seemed sunken, but they blazed with a fierce intensity at the white-faced man on the bed. "It's bad," she said, lips stiff. "I know that. But how bad, Doctor Cordell?"

Cordell looked up at her under red, shaggy brows as he went about sterilizing transfusion equipment. "I don't believe in feeding false hopes," he said heavily. "If it were any other man, he'd already be dead."

"There's no chance?" Nita's voice was utterly expressionless.

Cordell belched out a laugh. "With Dick Wentworth, no man can say that. He makes his own chances!"

THROUGHOUT THE long days that followed, Wentworth made his chances, once in a long while opening his eyes upon Nita's anxious, watching face. She had forgotten the world, forgotten everything except that this man was hers and that Death never for a moment left his bedside. They fought a bitter duel in which there were no rests, this invisible specter and the man who so often had summoned him to serve others....

It went on like that for three weeks. Then, suddenly, the danger of pneumonia had been fought off. But he was pitifully weak and wasted, and the drains were still in his wounds. That day, his burning eyes met Nita's and a weak, slight smile moved his lips....

Nita was jubilant as a child. Lines of care erased themselves from her face overnight and Dr. Cordell glared at her sardon-ically.

"I know I'm not supposed to ask questions," he said brusquely. "Dick once did me a service I can never repay. But what I mean to say is: when are you two going to get married?"

Nita smiled at him cheerfully. She could smile now that Dick was on the mend. But it was Wentworth who answered, his voice scarcely audible. "Quit bullying her, you scoundrel."

Nita moved quietly to the bedside and took his bone-thin hands in hers. Cordell snorted again.

When he had gone, Wentworth lay long staring at the ceiling, hands moving restlessly upon the bed covers. After the red pain and black nothingness, he could think again and his thoughts were not pleasant. He would be months rebuilding his health and strength. Even his nerve reactions would be slowed and in the life he led, no man less swift than the Spider had been could survive.

"I'll tell you all about everything in a couple of days," Nita promised gaily.

Wentworth smiled, lips hard and withdrawn. "What good will it do?" he asked bitterly. "I'm helpless, and will be for weeks. Even when I leave the bed, there'll be little I can do...."

"Jackson and Ram Singh!"

Wentworth's hand moved impatiently. "Good men but lacking in initiative—in imagination."

Nita leaned over, brushed his hot forehead with tender lips. "You're to sleep now, dear. Remember that, though there can't be two Spiders, there is a... *a Spider's mate!*"

Wentworth's hand closed firmly about hers and the pitiful weakness of his grasp stabbed at her breast. "My... mate!" he whispered. "No, darling, not you. You must not enter this fight. You are too precious to me. Some day I must make you truly... my mate." His voice was strengthening. "You shall be. I swear it!" BUT WHEN he learned the true state of affairs, the overwhelming success of the suicide wave, it left Wentworth lying white and still on his bed. He had been consoling himself with the knowledge that the secret of the drug had been given to Kirkpatrick. That should have made it impossible for water systems anywhere to spread the madness that meant self-destruction. But they had. At least, the water continued to show the purple precipitate, and the deaths mounted by leaps and bounds—as if in punishment of those who dared fight.

New York now was only one plague spot among many. Death strode across the land with seven-league boots. Each skeleton footprint destroyed hundreds. Whole sections of the Middle West had been abandoned entirely; factories had shut down as their men fled the first invasions of the suicide death. Now and again, the name of Jackson Grant cropped up, and in its wake the toll of dead mounted widely. One of his mad feasts of Anubis ended in a wholesale suicide aboard an excursion boat. Men and women hurled themselves over the rails and for days afterwards, their water-mauled bodies drifted ashore. Two-hundred-fifty-seven died in that single disaster. But Grant's greatest attempt was a tenement fire. Into a great gaunt building more than five hundred had crowded to chant the hymn to Anubis while the flames crept in around them.

Captain Jorgensen had been seized in Chicago and put under observation in a psychopathic ward. But he had broken out of there by beating off his guard's head with an iron chain. The *Plutonic's* former physician, Doctor Masters, was drawing down a fat salary as advisor to the state of Arizona, where the suicide mania had struck with wanton savagery.

Craft Elliott was donated huge sums for use by Sneed Jenkins in preventive work which seemed to accomplish nothing. All of those whom Wentworth had suspected even fleetingly were there in the news—all of them except Jamid Bey.

When Nita had finished with her efficient digest of the news. Wentworth dragged a thin hand across his forehead.

"Nita," he said slowly, "I want Jackson Grant. He is the key to the whole thing, no question of that. Tell Ram Singh and Jackson to bring him to me."

Nita nodded, her eyes keen and happy. There was new vitality in this wasted man she loved, a new strength. He was back again at his work, at the duty to which he had pledged himself. It did not matter that he requested and expected of two men what the secret service of the nation and all the municipal police force were attempting vainly to accomplish. Nita laughed.

She stood stiffly and saluted, executed a neat right-about. "Right away, major!" she called back.

Wentworth lay staring at the ceiling, hands moving restlessly through the clippings of newspapers scattered across the bed. Tomorrow, he would sit up for the first time since he had whirled to the challenge of the policeman's cry and deliberately pulled his gun's muzzle high. And because he had spared that life, thousands more had died. His lips twisted in mockery. That was foolish, of course. There was no guarantee that the Spider could have stopped the carnage….

He felt a stinging in his eyes. Could any man be so well served? Jackson and Ram Singh and… and dear Nita! But it was not enough. No, the Spider must return to the battle, else this slaughter would go on and on endlessly until the streets were depopulated and men scurried about like fearful rats….

He knew that Nita had kept certain things from him. Nita had made no mention of the last worshipful gathering in the Temple of Anubis. Wentworth pushed his body up shakily on his arms, propped up his head with pillows, and fumbled the clippings. He found the story finally.

Of the fifty who had been arrested in that false temple, forty-six had committed suicide in their cells. Wentworth cursed savagely. He had accomplished nothing at all, nothing. Jackson Grant had eluded his grasp then, and was likely to do so now. How could he hope that Jackson and Ram Singh, able though they were, would succeed where all the enforcement agencies of the nations had failed?

Jackson Grant, the items said, was Public Enemy Number One. They would not rest until he was in their hands. But how many thousands would die before that time! God give strength and judgment to the Spider!

## CHAPTER 13
## THE SPIDER'S MATE

NITA GAZED fixedly at herself in the neon-lighted mirror as Jackson sent the Daimler hurtling toward New York City. Ram Singh's keen faithful eyes studied her, too. He leaned forward, touched the tip of a grease-pencil to the corner of Nita's right eye, then showed his white teeth in a smile.

"*Wah! Missie sahib!* Even I who know would swear thou art the Spider himself!"

Nita moved the stiff lips that had been built over her own in what was meant for an appreciative smile. The result made her shudder. Then she laughed. There was a gaiety in her tonight. Dick was mending; his mind could turn again to the matters which had harassed him. Her laughter faded quickly. With a sharp gesture, she signaled Ram Singh to close the wardrobe beneath the seat. He obeyed, crouched, swaying, on the floor, his eyes dreamy with happiness.

Back in his hills village, men would have laughed at Ram Singh and spat upon his turban—led by a woman! But Ram Singh, swaying, with the battle glint in his eyes, was content. They did not know such women as these. Fighters they knew, yes. Women who could do fierce, cruel things with a knife when the battle was raging. But not such a one as this, with the sharp, sure challenge of command in her voice, with a brain that leaped to the proper strategy more certainly than his own. And without doubts.

Nita stretched out her legs man-fashion in the man's suit

138

she wore, adjusting her mentality and her movements to the disguise. She smoked and it was a mannish gesture, stripped of her delicacy. As did Wentworth himself, so did Nita. Whatever disguise he wore, he became the person he portrayed. And so must Nita herself. When she spoke, Ram Singh started and jerked his mind from his dream. It was the flat, menacing voice of the Spider that had addressed him. And Nita leaned back, smoking, satisfied.

*The Spider's mate,* she had called herself. More deadly than the male. She laughed bitterly. Heaven give her the strength, the courage, and the intelligence to carry through tonight. Let her not bring dishonor to this black cape and the black hat upon her wigged head. About one thing she need not fear. She could shoot with the snaky quickness of the Spider himself. Not with his unvarying accuracy, but better than most… much better. Dick had seen to that. She might feel doubts, but never fear.

The Daimler slowed to a stop, and at a gesture from Nita, Ram Singh sprang to the door.

"Remember," she said harshly, "thou art to follow. No more. Or I'll trim off those unheeding ears of thine with the toy thou callest a knife."

Ram Singh's white teeth flashed joyously as he swept a low salaam, cupped hands rising to his forehead.

*"Han, sahib!"*

He was gone, mingling with the shadows. It was a lone trail she followed, and it might be a long one. Denver Dane, as well as Helen Stuyvesant, had survived the affair at which Wentworth had fallen. He had fled in time from the temple of Anubis. So far, the Spider's menace had shocked them from renewing their association with the mad congregation of Jackson Grant. But Nita was sure that soon Dane, at least, would turn that weak face of his toward the worship that had seized on him with insatiable hands. She knew not by what secret means he learned of such things, but in someway he would know where to attend the meetings of Jackson Grant....

THE WAIT that followed was wearying and fruitless. Three days and nights went by—days in which the only joy was Dick's increasing strength. But on the fourth night, Nita finally got the clue she sought. Dane had gene to a splendid mansion on upper Riverside Drive, and into the same door, dozens of others found their furtive way.

Nita was content then to wait. Not for her the daring invasions of the Spider, the attempt to dominate assemblies of suicide-crazed men and women.... For four hours she smoked cigarettes end-to-end. Then Ram Singh came flying back, breath quick and loud in his nostrils.

"A hundred men and women, *missie sahib!*" he cried softly. "They march forth behind Jackson Grant!"

Something like despair gripped Nita then. This was not what she had planned, what she had hoped....

"Follow," she said crisply. "And be this Jackson Grant thy special charge, O warrior. Let him not once from thy sight and when he has come to rest, give word to Jenkyns—or seek me out if I be near."

Ram Singh hesitated; gazing into the mock-face of the man he loved and served. "And thou, *missie sahib?*"

She fired in sharp succession at the charging *fellaheen!*

If anything happened to this woman and he protected her not, the grief of his master would be upon his head. After all, she was woman....

"Coward!" Nita's voice was scornful. "Wouldst have a woman do thy work!"

Anger leaped like a knife into the Hindu's eyes, then once more his teeth flashed.

"Give salaam. I hear and obey!"

He was gone, a shadow in the darkness. Nita caught up the speaking tube, spoke to Jackson. "A hundred fools are marching out to kill themselves, Jackson, It's up to us to stop them somehow and make Grant run for it. Then Ram Singh will follow him. Follow their march until we can determine what to do."

Jackson sent the long car stealthily forward. "I could charge them, miss—with the car?"

"No," Nita said. "Not that."

"Might shoot over their heads, miss?"

Nita said nothing. She sank back against the cushions. Dick was right. These two were brave, but without imagination. Death would follow on the heels of either attempt, death and failure. And Nita wanted mightily to live now. When all this was over, Dick would have to go away somewhere to rest. If she could only smash this Suicide League before Dick was well enough to put himself in danger again....

But this was no time for dreaming. Up there, a hundred souls marched eagerly to their doom. She could hear the swelling vigor of their chant. Police would try to stop them, doubtless, but guns were of no avail against those who wished only to die; nothing less than death or unconsciousness would stop them.

AND SUDDENLY the horror of it all gripped Nita. These were human beings! These creatures, who moved with a swinging stride that held a joy worthy of greater things; were men and women who loved and struggled: girls who yesterday a week ago, had stood behind the counters of some store or tapped a typewriter's keys, had ridden home in evening in a press of humans that made the subway sweltering, to dress excitedly for an evening at the neighborhood movie with the boy friend. There were men there too—a householder who a month before had spent the long summer twilights manicuring a patch of green lawn in Sunnyside. Had he no son? Was there no thought for him of a kid with his shirt tail flapping as he ran, and a knicker leg about his ankle, to put a pain in his breast and awake him? Of a woman toiling through the years beside him? *Good God!* Perhaps his wife walked beside him!

Nita thrust emotion from her and once more studied the serried throng that marched chanting to its death. How was it possible to stop them? The thin, mewling wail of a police siren reached her ears. Or was it the police? Did they even try now to check those who would kill themselves? Nita's lips curved. Probably the fire department.... She laughed sharply, leaned forward and rapped on the glass. When she spoke, her voice had the crackling temper of the Spider.

"Find a fire-house, Jackson," she ordered, "we're going to steal a fire truck!" She caught Jackson's eye in the rear-vision mirror

143

and he grinned. "The major'll get a kick out of this, miss," he said. "How'll we work it?"

They swung a corner with whining tires, spotted the open doors of a fire-house, blue-shirted men lolling in their shirt sleeves before it. Nita's eyes were sharply excited now and she ignored the high, unsteady hammering of her heart. Jackson's approval gave her a renewed courage.

"Stop just beyond it, leave the engine running and the door open." She was talking briskly now, without hesitation. "I'll stand them off. You drive the truck out and stand by with a gun in your hand until I get to the car. Then both of us drive as fast as we can for the corner of Riverside Drive and One Fifty-Fifth Street."

Jackson protested, "But, Miss...."

Nita swung from the door, walked with long man-strides toward the firemen before the house. The cape of the Spider fluttered from her shoulders and in her hands glinted the Spider's guns.

"Inside!" she rasped, and it was the Spider's voice, too, that grated out from between disguised lips. "Inside, fools, and—" Her right-hand automatic blasted flame and lead, chipped bricks above the head of one—"don't make any mistakes!"

THE ECHOES of the shot blasted along the quiet street, dropped a blanket of fear over the three men before the house. The tilted chair of one wavered wildly, slammed him down on his back. He rolled, bounced up with his hands in the air.

"The Spider!" he wailed. "Oh, God, the Spider!"

Already Jackson was racing past the trembling men. Seconds

later, he wheeled a hose truck out into the street, jerked to a halt and stood waving a gun.

Nita said levelly, "It's quite all right, men. You'll find the truck shortly, unharmed." She ran to the Daimler, whose license plates had been covered by a skillful device of Wentworth's own contriving, slammed in gear and got smoothly under way. An instant later, the hose truck's engine bellowed and together the two vehicles raced with rocketing, increasing speed down the narrow street, whirled off into the Avenue beyond. Jackson started the siren moaning. Nita gave him the lead, burned northward after him.

Traffic was scanty, but what there was gave their siren-cleared path a wide berth. In an incredibly short time, Jackson, the loud scream of the siren silenced, cut his lights and drifted down to the corner of the Drive she had designated.

Nita halted fifty feet behind him, spun the Daimler about and pointed it in the opposite direction. Then she ran on swift feet to where Jackson trailed lengths of hose from the truck. Nita caught up the wrench, bent over the fire-plug Jackson had picked. It was the work of moments to uncap a vent. The hose was connected and they two crouched in the darkness, waiting, listening. The hymn of Anubis was very near....

Straining her sight down the dim Drive, Nita could make out the compact, dark mass of marching men and women. She tried to distinguish whether Jackson Grant still strode at their lead, but she could not see, nor could she yet determine whether his deep, rolling voice still dominated the others. Where were they going, these mad ones? What new kind of death did they

145

seek? The first ranks passed a street light a block away and Nita's breath made a sharp noise between her teeth.

Jackson turned toward her, grinning, his eye corners crinkled: "Still there, ain't he? It'd be a cinch to take him now. Don't see how he's kept clear all this time."

"There are gunmen," Nita murmured. "Always at least six, the newspapers say. They hide among the innocent people and, naturally, that makes it rather difficult for the police. It won't be easy for us."

She let the wrench hang on the water lever and slipped out Wentworth's two heavy guns.

Jackson said sardonically, "Glad I'm on your side, miss. I'd better knock down Grant first, eh?"

"Yes, then break up the marchers as much as possible. Put it in their faces, Jackson. I think the singing makes them a little mad," Nita thrust the right-hand gun into her belt, caught hold of the water lever again. "The effective range of the hose is about fifty feet."

"Just about that." Jackson was enjoying himself. His great, wide shoulders were hunched against the expected thrust of the water in the hose. "Say when, Miss Nita."

As they crouched, waiting, a figure stole out of the shadows and Ram Singh salaamed before Nita.

"Your orders, *missie sahib?*"

NITA SHOOK her head. "Stand by in the shadows. We've going to try to break up the crowd with the hose. Try to knock out Grant. There'll be shooting and I don't want you hurt—any of us. Master Dick depends on us. When the chance comes, Ram Singh, *bring Jackson Grant to me!*"

Once more came the flash of white teeth and the salaam. Ram Singh merged with the shadows.

The chanting was very close now, very near the three in the dark of the side-street. Nita grasped the wrench. "Grant first," she whispered sharply, feeling the surge of strange power.

"Right!"

With a sweeping turn, Nita threw the current of water on full force. For an instant, air and the high-pressure stream gurgled in the nozzle. Nita saw Grant's gaunt, false face swing about, heard him shout and point a long, robed arm. The hose spat once, twice, burst into full strength as a revolver spoke from the thick of the crowd. Then the stream caught Grant full in the chest and face, bowled him from his feet, hurled him under the feet of those behind. Jackson's stream reached for the spot where the gun had blasted just as it spurted again.

Above the hiss and roar of the water, Nita did not hear Jackson grunt and sway an instant, then bear down harder than ever on the bucking hose. It was a two-man job. He braced his feet wide and leaned his powerful body into the task. Nita saw a man detach himself from the midst of the marchers, flee across the drive toward an open building of stone posts on the edge of the park. A gun lanced fire from his hand.

The chant broke, faltered as Jackson swung the hose slowly, battering men and women off their feet, rolling them into the gutters, seeking out killers behind the flickering flame of guns.

Nita's gun-sharp gaze swept the whole scene. A small group

of men moved from the main body; their faltering voices began to unite again. Nita touched Jackson's shoulder and pointed. The hose scattered them like a charging chariot. A gunman lunged for the protection of a tree that flanked the street and Nita fired twice before he fell. She was killing—killing with the deadly precision of the Spider himself—and she felt only a fierce, mounting joy in the deed. Later, remorse might rack her, but now she was defending her own, guarding these maddened people, making good for Dick. For unless she succeeded, Wentworth, ill and weak as he was, would take the field.

The wave of marchers fought again and again to reform ranks near the spot where Jackson Grant had fallen.

"Watch it, Ram Singh!" Nita's voice rose clear. "I want Grant!"

The stream of the hose rose high, over the heads of the crowd for a moment, then sloshed down upon them again. Nita sprang to Jackson's side, one gun thrust into her belt.

"I can… hold it." Jackson panted. His voice was muffled and Nita stared at him. His face was white and there was a dark stain at his left side. A cry rose in Nita's throat, uncertainty and dread clouded her brain. Jackson was wounded! She wanted to take him out of the battle, to take the hose and let him retire. But she knew she couldn't, knew she lacked the necessary strength. Not for a moment could she hold down the hose, nor could they stop now. Disaster in the first skirmish….

I can hold it!" Jackson repeated, more strongly, his voice harsh….

NITA NODDED and her gun was in her hand again. Her joy was replaced by a burning hate. A man, ducking close to the

148

ground, raced toward them, gun spitting. Nita felt lead tug at her cloak and once more laughter rasped from her throat. She fired both automatics, and laughed to feel their bucking thrust against her slender wrists. The gunman was jerked up straight on his feet, hurled over backward by the powerful slugs that had struck him. He rolled over twice before he lay still.

Nita threw a swift glance over the Drive and up the hill toward darkened, upper Broadway. Suddenly she was aware of a new sound—the whine of sirens. Police were coming, and she had slain—slain in the cloak and the name of the Spider! But the march was broken. Here and there, men reeled drunkenly on their feet, disorganized, no longer chanting. Ram Singh darted to her side, panting, fury writhing on his face.

"He is gone!" he cried. "The tall one fled with two men. My knife found one, but they reached a car. They go westward!"

"Help Jackson!" Nita commanded. "He's wounded." She cut off the flow of water with a swift pull of the wrench, raced for the Daimler. She saw Jackson sway as the pressure of the hose diminished, saw Ram Singh leap to his side. Then she was in the big sedan, whose engine she had left running. She slammed into reverse, rocketed backward to pick up her two men. They came at a pounding run, Ram Singh's right arm bracing Jackson. The instant they lunged into the tonneau, Nita had the Daimler under way. Its roar drowned out the rush of the sirens.

She was aware of a voice in her ear—Ram Singh talking through the speaking tube. "It was a sedan, *missie sahib,* but a small one, in which Grant fled. They were but entering it when

I came for you, but they were too far away for me to reach. Turn south, *missie sahib*, and…!"

Nita's attention wrenched from the voice to the scene ahead. Slamming around the corner, racing nose-on for the Daimler was a light coupé. For an instant, she thought it a police radio-car. Then she recognized another fact—the driver of the coupé was making no effort to swerve, to dodge the heavy, on-rushing Daimler!

And in that fleeting instant, Nita knew the truth. A madman, bent on suicide, had been sent to stop the Spider! Even as the realization flashed into her brain, the coupé roared with an extra burst of power, seemed to leap from the ground in a frantic lunge toward Nita's car!

## CHAPTER 14
## DEATH TAKES A TAXI

IN A brief, meteoric flash, Nita saw the wreck of all her plans, the doom of Richard Wentworth and everything he hoped to accomplish. This was his car—his two men servants—and she was wearing the Spider's disguise. Even if the crash did not kill them, it would deliver them into the hands of police or killers. Death and defeat raced toward her in that maniac-driven coupé. But there was no despair in Nita's soul. Defiant laughter burned her throat. Was she not the Spider's mate? She would burst free of this deadly trap!

She could not dodge the on-rushing car, not with its driver determined on collision. The only thing she could do was to strike in the way least damaging to herself. That would be nose-on, with all the heft and thrust of the Daimler driving in against the lighter coupé, which it outweighed tremendously. But it was not easy. The Daimler was climbing steep, rough hill that gave it poor traction. The coupé had the drive of gravity to lend it speed....

Her slim chances made Nita laugh again. She slammed into second gear, standing on the accelerator and the Daimler's speed mounted with the roaring of its mighty motor.

"Steady for crash!" she shouted as the two cars bounded to the meeting. She had time to be glad that Dick had only bulletproof glass and to think that he would be proud of her; she had time to glimpse the white, set face of the mad driver, then....

The two cars reared to the meeting like two stallions screaming into battle. Nita was aware of an overwhelming din, the high, shattering crash of breaking glass that was not her own. The rending, tinny sound of ripping steel simultaneous with the stunning, slamming shock of the two bodies. In the midst of all that, she managed to keep her foot grinding down on the accelerator, though the collision hurled her heavily against the steering wheel, breaking the stiff brace of her arms and legs.

The Daimler snarled like an angry beast; the fat tires whined and dug at the roughened pavement. Then the heavier weight—the momentum and steady drive of the Daimler's roaring engine—drove it on. The coupé twisted about on its own length, beaten in part by that last swerving. It began a horrible end-over-end spin toward the curb. The coupé was rearing its crumpled nose and its crash-stripped side toward the sky in a roll that would complete its demolition. Nita did not see the finish though she heard the crash. The Daimler was past, streaking on like a charging bull. She manhandled the weaving sedan around the next corner, sped southward, little crazy laughing sounds of relief in her throat.

SHE CRIED at herself: "Stop that! Stop that now!" She eased her foot on the accelerator. She had no time to see what had happened to the Daimler, but the engine droned smoothly and it answered readily to the wheel. A deep breath helped to quiet the trembling that shook her.

"Ram Singh!" she called. "Come up here and take the wheel!"

The left-hand door opened instantly, held against the whip of the wind by the Hindu's lean, powerful hand, and moments later, he took the wheel from her grasp.

"Give salaam, *missie sahib!*" he cried in his harsh, nasal voice. "Thou art a warrior!"

"Find Grant's car and keep to its trail," she said, making her voice firm and confident. "Press them close, but don't wreck them. I want Grant alive!"

She slid open the glass between front and rear and climbed over, dropped on the seat beside Jackson. His left hand was pressed to his side and he was slumped low against the cushions. Nita whipped open a compartment in the back of the front seat and revealed a medicine chest.

"Can you get that coat off, Jackson?" she asked calmly as she selected bandages and iodine.

"Certainly," Jackson said, his voice firm. "Splendid work, Miss

Nita. If we don't get those scoundrels tonight, it won't be your fault. It will be ours. Your men are bunglers!"

"Nonsense!" Nita contradicted cheerfully, "I just happened to be driving. Now let's get at that wound."

Jackson's jaw set as the iodine bit into raw flesh. Feeling a little faint, Nita forced her hands to steadiness as she worked.

"Flesh wound," she announced cheerfully. "Glanced off one of those steel ribs you call bones and took a bit of flesh along with it."

Jackson gasped out. "Lucky thing they can't shoot like you, Miss."

Nita raped on a tight bandage, helped Jackson get into shirt and tunic again.

"This is a conspiracy," Nita told him cheerfully. "You and Ram Singh are trying to make me feel important." She was working, talking to hold herself steady. She dared not do anything else, lest the reaction of the battle and that last close crash overwhelm her. Inwardly, she was quaking, not with fear, but with its aftermath, relief. She could not give way. There was more of the same ahead.

Nita found herself longing fiercely for action, for something to do. She drew Dick's automatics from their holsters, methodically reloaded them. She thought belatedly that she should have shot that fool in the other car. It might have turned the nose of the coupé a little sooner. The thought made her frown, and she wondered suddenly how Dick could be so tender, so gay, so understanding when life demanded of him that he kill, kill, kill….

Jackson said steadily, "It looks as if Ram Singh had caught the trail."

"He'd better, the salaaming son of a gun." Nita said with more grimness than she knew. She looked ahead, saw that a small, green sedan was rocketing along, jouncing a bit wildly. Her lips—the lips of the Spider—curved eagerly. "Our springs are better," she said. "If he keeps to this rough street, we'll have them before long."

A mist began to obscure the windshield and Ram Singh started the window-wiper, swiping monotonously back and forth.

"Must have smashed something in the radiator," Jackson said. "That's steam."

Nita felt a sinking weight in the pit of her stomach. Was it always like this when the Spider fought, she wondered, disaster after disaster, death and threat at every turn? Conquest only by almost superhuman endurance, by clinging on to hope when every hope seemed gone?

**SHE NODDED** mechanically when Jackson thanked her for doctoring his side.

"I'm ready for another water fight now," he said cheerfully. But Nita knew he would be weak from loss of blood. She drew a flask of whisky from the medicine cabinet, passed it to him, heard his blown-out breath of happiness. "That'll fix me up proper!"

Because of the steaming radiator, Ram Singh closed the distance between the two cars in great rushing roars of speed. When finally the little sedan whirled from the rough street into a smoother one that led southward, they were a scant thirty feet apart. A gun began to flame in the forward car. Nita eyed its red spurts with a frowning brow, weighing her own heavy guns upon her knees. She couldn't kill. After all, this Grant was only an underling, Dick had told her. If he were allowed to go on, he might lead her to his master. But there wasn't time—not with the Daimler spouting steam like a locomotive.

"Change seats with me, Jackson," she ordered briefly. That done, she opened the window, leaned out with her gun. A bullet whined past her head as she pumped four evenly spaced shots at the other car, not high enough to hit anyone... The fourth shot did the trick. A tire let out a hissing scream and the green sedan swerved wildly. Ram Singh barely braked down in time before the other car cut erratically across his path, leaped the opposite curbing and nuzzled a stone wall that surrounded an imposing estate.

Nita stepped to the pavement, fresh gun poised in her right hand while Ram Singh raced forward, weaving in a crouch, a knife glinting in his hand.

"Alive! The tall one alive!" Nita shouted after him. "Jackson, take the wheel."

Even as Ram Singh reached the rear of the green sedan, she saw the tall priest of Anubis leap from the right-hand door and spring to the wall in a long, looping bound from the right fender. Her gun started up, but she held her fire while Ram Singh raced for the fugitive. A second man bobbed from the car, gun in his fist, but before he could fire, Ram Singh's knife flickered upward from his side, a beautiful, a perfect throw. It buried its glinting blade in the man's throat and he pitched forward.

With a long bound, the Hindu cleared the body of his prey, slipped as a convulsive movement of the dying gunman caught his flying feet. He recovered instantly, but that single moment had given Grant time to vanish over the wall. Scarcely a second behind him, Ram Singh leaped the barrier and disappeared too. Nita waited, listening, then sprang to the back seat.

"Cruise along the south wall," she cried sharply.

The Daimler rolled forward. Jackson paused for an instant to collect Ram Singh's prized knife. Then they were creeping onward.

Jackson said, "We'll have to have another machine."

"I'll take the wheel," Nita said shortly. "You should find a taxi within two blocks. Better buy it." She awkwardly took a wallet from a pocket, handed him a sheaf of bills. Jackson set off rapidly, but somewhat weakly. When he came back, she decided, he would have to dispose of the Daimler for her and get Dick's Hispano-Suiza roadster. A taxi did well enough in the city, but there might be work in the open country too.

JACKSON, RETURNING quickly with the cab, protested at the order to return the Daimler to the garage but he met a firmness before which he bowed. He climbed into the crippled Daimler.

"Get that wound treated at Doctor Cordell's office," Nita told him, as she climbed into the taxi, "after you get the Hispano. I'll call you there with directions for meeting us after we have Grant."

Jackson saluted, his grin wide again. By damn! She meant it, too! *After we have Grant!* No *if* about it at all! And she could make him jump. Never thought he'd jump again to any command but the major's.

"Get going!" Nita ordered impatiently. He saluted again, got going. The Daimler's engine was beginning to knock with heat.

Nita waited behind the wheel of the taxi, watching the dark walls and frowning. Ram Singh should be calling to her soon, or reporting. He... A gaunt, tall figure topped the wall laboriously, dropped to the pavement and crouched, sweeping the street with his eyes. He spotted the taxi, hesitated, then came toward it loping, holding up a finger. Nita's lips smiled, but her eyes were dark and hard.

She started the taxi with a jerk, flung the Spider's hat to the floor and pulled the taxi driver's cap down over her eyes. The cape was still on her shoulders, but the light would not be strong. It should pass unnoticed... She ran a little past Jackson Grant, let him open the door himself. Ram Singh was nowhere in sight. Above the wall, nothing stirred....

"Where to?" Nita made her voice gruff.

"Southward!" Grant's deep tones came. "Go down Park!"

Nita managed to slide an automatic from its holster and thrust it into her belt. Best be ready for emergencies, though she expected none. Jackson Grant made no sound in the rear seat and she kept the taxi droning at a good rate, pausing only for lights. In the Sixties, Grant said suddenly: "Turn right, and stop." Nita was warm with happiness, with the pleasure of work well done. When Jackson Grant left the taxi, she would take him prisoner and carry him to Dick and she would know also either his own hide-out or that of his masters. She had no doubts now. She had lived through a baptism of fire.

As she halted, Nita felt cold metal grind into the back of her neck.

"Next time, Spider." Grant said heavily, triumphant, "don't forget to pull down the flag of your taximeter. It makes passengers suspicious!"

## CHAPTER 15
## WHEN ENEMIES MEET

C HAGRIN, NOT terror, was Nita's first reaction to that gun pressed against her neck. She thought bitterly that Dick would not have forgotten the flag that set the taxi meter to working and she thought other hard, accusing things. She didn't have the courage, she jibed at herself, to snatch for the gun at her waist. Anger was sweeping her... She fought it down, battled against her despair. Anger was no more a means of controlling oneself than it was of ruling others. Moreover, rashness and courage were not the same. It would be rashness to grab for her gun now....

"My dear Grant," Nita said in the best Spider manner, "that was careless of me. So glad you called it to my attention."

With the gun on her, Nita climbed carefully, slowly to the pavement, removing the taxi driver's hat. "You won't mind if I get my own *chapeau*, will you? This one is quite a bit too small." Nita contrived to make her voice anxious.

Jackson Grant was eyeing her with dark, somber gaze, high narrow head bent forward a little. "I think we'd better leave it there," he said gently, "until I have an opportunity to take your guns. Now, face about, and...."

Nita did as he directed, walked toward the doorway before which the taxi stood. It was just a chance, of course, but Ram Singh might have topped the wall in time to see the taxi drive off. If he followed, the hat lying on the floor would identify the taxi and the house into which she had gone. The Hindu could follow such a trail as that. It was the work he did best, that and killing with his long, keen knives. Nita told herself these things to buoy her hope. With despair came hopelessness. What could she do?

A butler opened the door, bowing suavely, and they crossed a formal reception-room to an elevator operated by a dark-faced man clad in white, linen robes. And suddenly Nita knew where she would be taken next: the apartments of Jamid Bey! She was suddenly sure of this. For a moment, the crowding excitement of the discovery, the confirmation of the two bowing *fellaheen* when the elevator let them out into a lavish foyer, transcended her worry and her fears.

She knew that Wentworth had been convinced of Bey's innocence. Now the Suicide Priest brought her to his rooms! If only she could retain one of her guns. There was one in her belt, one in the holster beneath her arm... The *fellaheen* drew apart carpets from a doorway and somewhere within chimes sounded softly. The chamber was the same in which Wentworth had talked with Jamid Bey, the ceiling domed in blue, the walls a series of Moorish arches resting on slender spiraling columns. But it was the woman, Nephtasu, who looked up from where she knelt upon the cushions beside the tinkling fountain. Flame leaped up in her green eyes and her long, slim mouth smiled.

"What have you brought me now, my friend?" she asked softly, in her slurred, huskily full voice. Much as Nita detested the woman, she could not deny her beauty and charm.

"I dislike killing men," Grant said fluently, "and I thought some of your men might dispose of this for me. It is a vermin known as the Spider. You might also have them take his guns."

Nephtasu's green eyes swept over Nita. The smile stayed on her lips as she gave an order in beautiful Arabian. Nita caught the gist of it. Impossible to remain in Dick's company long and not grasp some of the many languages in which he was fluent. She herself was almost as much at home in French as English. German and Italian, she knew not quite so well… Nephtasu had ordered that her guns be taken.

Brown hands patted Nita's arms, her hips, found the holsters and took one gun. Nita's body shrank and quivered from the touch of those hands, but she did not permit herself to recoil, keeping her pose careless, her muscles hard. The *fellah* reported two holsters, one gun.

"The other gun, my dear," Nephtasu purred, "or shall I have you stripped to find it?"

NITA GAZED into the glowing green eyes and realized that her secret had been discovered. Nephtasu knew that she was a woman. But then, Nita had not expected otherwise. She gave this Egyptienne credit for keen intelligence, even though the sight of her made Nita's flesh crawl. Still, that gun was the only weapon between her and absolute surrender, absolute failure. So as to hide the automatic, she had managed to contract her stomach muscles just enough to let the heavy gun slip down inside her belt, so that the binding of the leather gripped its butt.

Thus it was not in a place where she could get at it swiftly. There were three men, Jackson Grant with the revolver he carried still leveled at her, the two *fellaheen* behind her, one of them with her other automatic... Nita's shoulders wanted to sag, but she held them back, shrugged gracefully. "Madame is indeed a pressing hostess."

"Courage is not foolhardiness, my dear," Nephtasu whispered.

Nita drew in a quivering breath, dropped the gun to the floor. Its thud was heavy. The crash of her own hopes, of Dick and peace, fell with it.

"I should apologize for such a juvenile trick," she said lightly, "but I did not expect such cleverness in Jackson Grant."

Nita actually laughed as Grant spluttered, stepped forward with a clenched fist. She could meet that attack. It might give her opportunity for escape! Nephtasu's sharp command halted him. "No, no, my friend," she said gently. "Surely you would not strike a... a defenseless man!"

Grant's narrow, long face was working. "Do you know what this defenseless man and his hirelings have done tonight?" he demanded bitterly. "I had persuaded a hundred fools to make a Golgotha out of a strip of Riverside Drive—to crucify themselves and this... this...!"

"Spare my innocence," Nephtasu murmured, "and let me hear your story."

Nita looked at Jackson Grant and thought. "Crucify themselves! I might have killed this murderer and I let him live. *Crucify...! I let him live!*"

Jackson Grant stepped backward a full pace, leveled the revolver in a hand that trembled slightly. "You move one finger and I'll kill you," he stammered. "I'll kill you!"

Nita had not moved a finger. She had merely looked at him with her wonder and her anger in her eyes.

"Well," Nephtasu interrupted sharply, "how much longer must I wait for my story?" She said it as a queen might command a slave. Nita looked at her narrowly, listened to Jackson Grant's recital of her attack and pursuit. While he talked, Nephtasu's eyes remained dreamingly on Nita with a cold appraisal in their depths that gave way slowly to admiration. But in them, Nita found nothing to inspire hope. Her desperation mounted. If she must die....

"And so, my friend," Nephtasu drawled when Jackson Grant had finished, "you wish me to remove this obstacle from your path?"

"At once!"

Nephtasu nodded. "I think you are wise. I should not care to have her feats reach the ears of the Bey—or there would be a new queen!"

Jackson Grant was frowning. "What are you talking about?"

"The lady you wish to kill, my friend."

Jackson Grant's mouth fell open. His hands shook as with a palsy. A woman!

NITA CAME out of her smiling pose in a flash of action. The gun was lax in the priest's hand and Nita had it in an instant, was standing facing the room, covering Grant and two *fellaheen* and Nephtasu.

"I have killed three men tonight," Nita said grimly, "and there may as well be others, or perhaps a woman. Nephtasu, please repeat that to your men. I know enough Arabic to see if you follow instructions." She waited while Nephtasu obeyed carelessly. Then she backed toward the door. "Grant," she said quietly, "walk backward toward me. You and I are going to take a little walk...."

Stumbling precipitately toward her, Jackson Grant tripped over a rug and his shoulders hit her. Nita's teeth clicked together and she lashed out with the revolver, caught Grant behind the ear. The two *fellaheen* sprang forward, knives flashing. Nita stepped coolly clear of Grant's falling body, fired twice in sharp succession. A vast coolness held her, succeeding her despair, and she cried out in triumph. Only Nephtasu now. She whirled, but before she could act, the Egyptian woman was upon her.

Such lithe, swift movement from the woman was so unexpected that Nita was driven back to the wall from the force of the attack. The two *fellaheen* were kicking out their lives upon the floor; Jackson Grant was unconscious at her feet, but Nephtasu...! Her two hands closed cleverly on Nita's gun wrist; violent pain stabbed the arm. Nita dropped the revolver, struck with her left hand. Not with a clenched fist—her weight and the strength of her wrist could not stand that—but with the first two fingers of her hand forked and stiff—straight at Nephtasu's eyes!

The Egyptienne dodged back, loosing her hold. The gun lay on the floor between them and the two women stood gazing at each other, panting a little—Nita with her woman's grace that had betrayed her despite the grotesque garb of the Spider; Nephtasu superb in one of those heavy silken gowns in which she delighted, a dress without decoration, simple of line so that her exquisite figure might show to its greatest advantage. The gown was a pale, apple green and her hair, piled above it, was a pillar of twisted fire.

It was Nita who advanced, lightly, alertly on the balls of her feet, her right arm slowly regaining sensation after the application of the paralyzing *jiu-jitsu* hold. Nita was adept at that art, too, for Wentworth had insisted on her learning it, just as he had the rudiments of fencing. Since she demanded—and he could not refuse—the right to share his dangerous life, it was best that she learn to defend herself ably....

Nephtasu awaited her coming with her pale lips still mocking, but with hatred in her eyes. "I shall break you before I kill you, fool!" she called slurringly. "That body of yours is too beautiful, and your face beneath that mask... Ah! *Ah!* Now I know you. Those eyes, I could not mistake them, I...!"

Nita sprang forward, feigning for a wrist grip, a hammerlock. She saw from the deft shifting of 'Tasu's muscles what her counter would be and struck swiftly for the chin with the heel of her hand. If it had landed, the blow would have jolted the Egyptienne's head backward on her shoulders and a swift slash with the edge of the other hand would have paralyzed the larynx, made her an easy prey.

Instead, Nephtasu snatched Nita's wrist, flung herself backward toward the floor, drawing her knees upward. She intended to jam those feet against Nita's body, whirl her with the momentum and leverage of the fall and smash her down, broken and helpless, perhaps dead. Only one defense against that. Nita must go with the fall, but work it to her own advantage. *Jiu-jitsu* is essentially an art of yielding, of defense. An expert can use the momentum and weight of his opponent's body to his own advantage, even as Nephtasu attempted now to use the force of Nita's rush in a throw that would increase her momentum and dash her terribly against the floor....

THE COUNTER to Nephtasu's attack was to permit the other woman to succeed in everything except one factor. She must not be able to release her hold upon Nita's wrist. If Nita held fast, balled instead of sprawling, the force of the throw could be used as momentum for a reversal against Nephtasu. But Nita doubted the strength of her arms for the purpose. She balled, held to Nephtasu's wrists just long enough and, catching the impetus of the thrust of the Egyptienne's feet, she turned an easy somersault in the air, landed on her feet, rolled once and came up alertly.

Nephtasu was rising lazily from the floor, sure of her conquest, and Nita's rush took her by surprise. She reeled backward from a forthright, unscientific thrust of both hands and pitched backward into the shallow tinkling fountain which formed the room's center. While she tumbled, splashing, Nita dashed for the revolver which had fallen. It was not in sight and there was no time to search. She sprang toward the fallen *fellaheen*, throwing a swift glance toward Nephtasu as she did so.

The Egyptienne, sitting in the fountain's basin in what should have been a ludicrous position, was in the act of throwing a knife. Nita ducked under the flying blade, but was compelled to whirl to face a new attack as Nephtasu sprang forward.

Nita let her eyes go wide with terror as the hating face of the Egyptienne neared her. Her head began to jerk frantically from side to side as if she sought escape. As Nephtasu, exultant, sprang toward her, Nita dodged aside, caught one of the woman's outreaching hands and spun on her heel. It was a clever throw, and perfectly executed. Nita's hands held for a moment, then slipped loose. Nephtasu, propelled by the force of her rush, was whirled about off-balance, tripped over Nita's dragging foot and flung spread-eagled, face down toward the floor.

Nita knew what must be done and she acted without hesitation. Completing her whirl upon her heel as Nephtasu struck with a muffled scream, she sprang bodily upon the Egyptienne's back and struck twice violently with the hard edge of her hand upon the back of her victim's neck. Then Nita reeled panting to her feet and Nephtasu lay where she had fallen, a bedraggled, half-nude woman in a wet torn dress, still lovely with the pile of her glorious hair streaming about her....

Nita could pause neither to admire, nor to gloat. Already too many swift moments had sped. She could not have many more before her enemies came. Sobbing for breath, she darted to the bodies of the Egyptian servants she had killed, found her automatic and holstered one as she ran to where Grant lay. He was already stirring and she slapped him heavily across the face....

"Get up, fool!" she rasped. "Get up before I fill you with lead!"

Grant's eyes opened and there was terror in them as he reeled to his feet, staggered toward the curtained exit of the suite. Nita felt a sharply rising exultation. She had made foolish mistakes and almost been trapped. But her enemies had been overconfident and mistaken, too. And she had triumphed. She had her prisoner. In the street, her car waited and she could take to Dick not only the man he must question, but information which might well fix responsibility for all the Suicide League's crimes. The answer was there in the suite of Jamid Bey, she was certain. But her brain was weary now, her body racked with the fatigue of mortal exertions. Dick would know the answers, Dick to whom she was going now....

THE ARMS closed about her from behind—men's arms that were bands of steel. The gun dropped from her paralyzed fingers. In quick succession, despair gripping her throat, Nita tried the only two tricks which might avail. She bent sharply forward and sideways to throw the man who held her prisoner over her hip... and it failed. He was too strong for that. She went lax and used her dead weight as a drag upon those gripping arms, but that, too, failed. The arms only closed more tightly until her breath came gasping through her mouth.

The man who held her laughed. "There, there, my dear! It is not polite for a guest to leave before the host's return. Especially when the guest is so lovely and efficient a lady."

The arms tightened still more and Nita felt herself lifted

and carried backward. She heard Grant's voice crackling with rage, and the easy laughter of her captor. The pressure upon her lungs made her dizzy. The room, the motionless figures on the floor swam.

Blackness swooped upon her….

## CHAPTER 16
## THE CAMP OF DISASTER

FOR LONG after Nita left him the fourth day, Wentworth studied the clippings which freshly confirmed his worst fears of the terror that had reigned after his fall. And he could do nothing but wait for others to do his work! Finally, his head nodded and he slept, until the sharp ringing of the telephone beside the bed roused him. He smiled bitterly at the unusual weight of the instrument in his weak hand. But even self-mockery deserted him as he listened to the rapid, harsh Hindustani of Ram Singh.

Finally, Wentworth let the phone rest on the bed, his hand weary of its weight, and stared straight ahead of him with stony eyes. Brave Nita, seeking to carry out his work while he lay helpless had fallen into the hands of the enemy, a prisoner of Grant! No other interpretation to put on her having walked into the Carlston ahead of him, just as there could be no doubt that he had taken her to the apartments of Jamid Bey, upon whose honesty Wentworth had once staked his life!

Wentworth's hands closed once, slowly, drily, then he picked up the phone again. "Nothing to do but wait and watch, Ram

Singh," he instructed heavily. "On no account allow yourself to be seen, or attack to free the *missie sahib*. We must learn their plans first of all. Do you know where Jackson is?"

Jackson had not been captured with Nita, Ram Singh was positive. When the Hindu had left the phone, Wentworth sat staring at his thin, useless hands. There was a tortured incredulity about his eyes. Never before had Nita fallen into the hands of the enemy and he been unable physically to go to her help, or to attack her captors. The calmness of his voice had not betrayed him, but the pain of this last blow was a crushing weight upon his enfeeble shoulders.

It was fifteen minutes later that Dr. Cordell telephoned. "This fool sergeant of yours has got himself shot with a garlic bullet," he said sharply. "The wound isn't bad, but there's an absolute certainty of septicemia unless strenuous steps are taken at once. Stop that laughing, you fool! There's nothing to get hysterical about."

WENTWORTH STOPPED the broken laughter. "Of course there isn't," he agreed, and laughed again. "No, no, it's quite all right, Cordell. I have complete control over myself. You must take the best of care of Jackson. Yes, we do have rather a knack for picking up bullets. Good morning."

Wentworth bit down the laughter that rose in his throat. It wasn't healthy. He pushed back the covers from his lank height and dragged his feet toward the floor. They weighed tons each. The Negro man who had been engaged as nurse opened the door a crack and came in making soothing motions with his hands.

"Now there, Mr. Wentworth, suh, you can't do nothin' like that. You can't do it. Not for a week, suh."

Wentworth grinned thinly at him. "Look here, nurse, don't try to tell me anything."

"You ain't goin' nowhere, Mr. Wentworth, suh," George said earnestly, his black, kinky head wagging. "You just *can't!*"

Wentworth kept looking at him. George moved his big feet uneasily, finally turned away, brought clothing. He was a giant of strength, with his broad, thick-chested body and narrow hips. His hands were wonderfully gentle as he helped Wentworth dress.

"Now, what you goin' to do, suh?" Wentworth lay back on the bed and rested for long moments, eyes on the ceiling, chest panting with weakness.

"I'm not quite sure, George, but I'll expect I'm going to make your fortune."

"My fortune, suh? My fortune?"

Wentworth could hear the Negro's wide grin in his voice. "Yes, George. I can't walk, you see, so you'll have to carry me, pick-a-back probably. It would be worth five thousand or so to you to do it."

"Five thousand *dollars,* suh?"

"Five thousand dollars, George."

"Yas, *suh,* Mr. Wentworth, suh. I'd carry you to the moon and back for that, suh. 'Deed I would."

**IT WAS** hours past dark when Ram Singh phoned again. Nita, with Grant, Nephtasu, Jamid Bey and a large retinue had boarded two planes at Newark airport, privately chartered for a trip to Mojave, Arizona. Wentworth frowned, bewildered by the move, but his orders were swift. Ram Singh should engage a large cabin plane and a pilot, land as near Wentworth's cottage hide-out as possible. He must procure a vast quantity of bulletproof silk, modeling clay and a papier-mâché which was self-drying and required no heat process, and certain radio equipment… It was three hours before the Spider's plane took off to trail the others. Wentworth set Ram Singh to work on the materials he had bought, then went to sleep. He must husband his strength for the trial to come….

The strong bumping of the plane awoke Wentworth and he peered out of the port to find that they were skimming the tops of dense clouds that momentarily lifted higher. Before them rose a towering thunderhead, laced through with the jeweled fire of lightning. Wentworth made his way laboriously with the help of the Negro, George, to the pilot's cockpit, noting as he went that their altitude was above eight-thousand feet. The pilot's face was set, his grin sardonic.

"The report said, local thunder showers." He yelled, "The whole damned Mississippi valley is like this."

As he spoke, he was winging southward to avoid the thunderhead in their course. A buffeting wind sent them scudding erratically, with a lurch that almost threw Wentworth. The plane was climbing steeply and cold was seeping into the craft, not intended for altitude flying. Even so, the clouds climbed still more rapidly and the plane changed course again to avoid another thunderhead.

"Ceiling zero down under," the pilot shouted again.

Death was very close to them all now—far out on the desert sands!

Wentworth dropped into the co-pilot's seat, strength wavering, and bucked the crash strap, put on radio head-phones. The pilot shot him a curious glance. He knew his passenger. Few were the major airports where his lean, striding figure wasn't familiar. His flying skill was a thing of which experts spoke respectfully.

The plane was bucking wildly, far beyond Wentworth's strength to control. He could not hope to take over, but if he could get a radio signal, they might ride the storm down. They had to. Within moments; the plane would have reached its ceiling; then the clouds would smother it. They would fly blindly and the first thunderhead they met would....

Wentworth's lips twitched once as he leaned forward, working the dials. So much depended on this little thing—the finding of a minute sound in the midst of all this turmoil. Life was at stake, of course, but there was much more than that. Nita's future, the welfare of the nation and the defeat or triumph of the Suicide League. All these flew the skies today.

The radio beam signals of a landing field sang into his ear, were lost and found again as he twirled the direction finder. He looked up at the pilot, smiling. "The course is due south," he said, making himself heard with difficulty. "Delron City Field." HE SAT back in the seat, eyes closed, listening to the fade and rise of the signal. The smother of clouds was all about them, shredding over the wings, smearing past the cockpit glass. The ship rocked violently. Their troubles were far from ended. Even when they found the field, landing on an unknown location in this black smother would be almost impossible. Wentworth gathered strength for that emergency.

Southward through the fury of the skies they sped while Ram Singh labored at the task set him and the Negro, with the novelty of flight worn off, dozed in complete ignorance of what threatened. The signal grew so strong finally that Wentworth removing the ear-phones and hanging them on their peg still could hear the sound.

"Must be getting near, sir," the pilot shouted.

Wentworth nodded, glanced out along the wings. He could see a vague haze of color—the running lights necessary even by daylight. Visibility less than fifty feet; altitude fifteen hundred! A weather report began to come in and Wentworth took up the phones again. An end of the fog and storm was expected by the next noon. Wentworth's lips moved slightly. It might as well last till doom's day, in that case. Their gasoline had been reduced by the battle with winds. An hour's fuel was all that was left.

"Land at Delron City," the pilot shouted.

There was no choice at all. It was that, or grope on until the fuel was exhausted, then grope for anything that might lie below. Practically certain death. But Delron City was five hundred miles from Mojave—five hundred miles that would take fifteen hours of frantic driving over treacherous roads, even if the fog let up. With the fog… Wentworth's heart was heavy as he helped the pilot to spot the field.

A jagged rip of lightning flashed past the nose of the ship. The plane heeled, staggered, dived wildly. Five hundred feet from the earth, the pilot pulled it out again. The radio was dead.

Rain drummed savagely, fiercely, over the metal cabin. For brief seconds, the shredded clouds broke below them and Wentworth, peering eagerly, glimpsed the yellow window-glow of a farmhouse, a rolling spread of corn fields.

He signaled sharply for the controls, pushed the ship down in an almost vertical dive. The motors drummed to a higher pitch and wind shrieked past the cabin. Wentworth's ears popped with the changing pressure, but he aimed directly for the cornfields below, fighting to get down before the thick weather closed in on them again. The altimeter hand swept over, three hundred, two hundred, one….

Wentworth snapped out of the dive, swung in a steep bank, and visibility was zero again! Nevertheless, he continued the bank until the nose was where he wanted it, leveled off and felt for the ground.

"I'll pay the damages," he said in the quiet of cut motors.

"Pay hell!" the pilot grunted, "if you just get me down alive…!"

Corn tops came spearing up out of the fog, brushing the undercarriage. The plane's landing lights showed the boiling white of the mist; then black out of the darkness, a huge gaunt barn rose in their path. Wentworth grabbed for the throttle, but the motor choked and died. Desperately, he hauled back on the mushy controls. The heavy ship raised loggily, began to settle, smashed nose on into the barn. With his last conscious thought, Wentworth reached out and cut the ignition… There was a great, black rending of timbers; then an overwhelming avalanche of furious sound—and darkness….

# CHAPTER 17
# BRIDE OF ANUBIS

MOJAVE LAY in the embrace of the Madres hills, which thrust out brown, withered arms on each side as if to hold back the invading sand waves of the desert. A small river romped down the valley, meandered through the midst of the homes, wandered out into the desert again and died there, sucked up in the monstrous heat. Fifty thousand souls made this hell their living place.

This was where the Egyptienne brought Nita and all her suite, setting the planes down in the sandy desert margin that served Mojave as a landing field. There were thousands there to greet them and, even as the ships touched earth, other thousands raced forth. Jackson Grant on the steps of one plane boomed out exhortations. The thousands responded—with the hymn to Anubis!

Nita saw these things with a sense of overwhelming dread. Her disguise had been stripped from her and her attire was modishly becoming. Nephtasu stood just behind her, laughter in the long green eyes.

"An excellent place to die, don't you think?" she murmured into Nita's ear.

"As good as any," Nita shrugged. She was not bound, or under restraint except for the two armed *fellaheen* who stood just behind her.

There was no sun now. Clouds hid the tops of the Madres and there was the distant thunder dance of lightning, but no

177

promise of rain. It seemed to Nita that nature, too, joined in the chant to Anubis... She was led hurriedly to an isolated house and as she and Nephtasu and the guards entered, thousands and ever new thousands marched past, each troop behind its scarlet-robed priest; each group chanting the song that had become the dirge of a nation.

"In heaven's name," Nita cried to the Egyptienne, "what deviltry are you planning here?"

Nephtasu's slim, pale lips curved sardonically. "You should ask in hell's name," she mocked. "We but prepare the town for the feast of Anubis in which you are to be especially honored."

Nita's face blanched white, but her sunken, violet eyes regarded Nephtasu unswervingly. "Which means?"

Nephtasu laughed lightly and the sound was more fearful than the chant of the fools outside. She turned away without answering, left the room with her slow, lithe tread. When Nita would have followed, the two *fellaheen* barred her way, thrust her into a room.

The door shut sullenly. Nita turned from it to the room's one window, which was barred. The scene outside continued unvarying. Men and women and children were trooping past behind scarlet-robed priests, singing, singing... The chant of it surged at Nita's brain endlessly, like the drumming of savage tom-toms. She bit her lips, clenched her white hands into fists. If they did not stop it soon, she would go mad. She flung herself across the bed....

NITA HAD no idea what time it was when she lifted her head again, but a nameless cold terror had her by the heart, made her shoulders quiver. A sob rose into her throat against all the resistance of her will and she closed her eyes with her terror, the last shreds of hope, of defense evaporated like steam.

At that moment, more than five-hundred miles to the north, Wentworth's plane crashed.

Nita could not have known that, yet before that time, hope had been her unfaltering companion. Now… nothing.

After a great while, she slept again, awoke to find Nephtasu standing over her. For a moment, Nita was not sure she was awake for the woman's garb was no longer her own interpretation of the current style. It had the barbaric, dazzling splendor of ancient Egypt. Her vivid hair was drawn back simply from the brows and caught up in back to fall in cascades over her shoulders. About her temples was the cobra-sun fillet of the Pharaohs. The rest of her costume was a double handful of some transparent silk that hung from an enormous, jeweled girdle low upon her hips. Her breast plates, a goddess might have envied. Upon her shapely arms were spiral bracelets, set with rubies and emeralds, made into the likeness of snakes. Nephtasu smiled and no longer was there mercy or gentleness in her expression. Civilization had been stripped from her with her clothing. Nothing remained but stark cruelty.

"I can see envy in your eyes, my dear," she purred, "but never fear, you shall dress just as splendidly for the feast of Anubis!"

She struck her hands together and a half dozen women, attired in scarlet like the priests, but without head-dresses, entered with obsequious gestures, bearing silken cushions on which lay garments of gossamer and jewels and precious metals beside which even those of Nephtasu paled into insignificance.

Little green fires burned in the Egyptienne's eyes. "Do you wonder that your splendor shall be even greater than that of the queen of Egypt?" she murmured. "The answer shall be yours, soon. Very soon!" She left the room, all lovely grace, and Nita watched her somberly… She submitted indifferently to the ministrations of the priest-women who stripped her glorious body with little cooing sounds of pleasure and excitement and praise.

She smiled bitterly at her reflection in the full-length mirror that was brought for her.

"Is it permitted that I know the purpose of all this?" she asked with gentle irony.

A priestess smiled on her, a toothless old woman with a gnarled face like a man's, smiled and winked. "What else," she cooed, "what else but that you are to be the bride of Anubis?"

NITA LOOKED at her without understanding. Then she laughed a little brokenly, turned from these old women in scarlet, turned again and looked at her reflection in the mirror and mocked the lovely image she saw. The bride of Anubis! She who aspired only to be the Spider's mate. Well, they would see today how a woman could die….

The priestesses came for her two hours later when the sun was burning down from a brazen sky. For an hour, there had been a constantly deepening volume of singing about the house. Nita was inured to it now, but her sense had not lost their acuteness. There was a new madness in the chant, a shrill-edged quality that told of the hysteria that gripped the frenzied victims of the conspirators.

As Nita, surrounded by the crimson ranks, walked toward the door, her head held proudly, her soul despairing, there was a fanfare of brazen trumpets—silence. Then, as she appeared, a vast inchoate shout that beat upon her with the physical violence of ocean waves. She looked about slowly. In every direction, flowing around houses, filling streets and yards, was the crowd, a tossing ocean of white faces with open, roaring mouths. Before her was a scarlet decked gangplank and at its other, end....

Nita lifted her eyes to the heavens and laughed, not very steadily—utterly unheard even by herself in the crazy crashing of voice-sound. Upon a platform which fifty men carried on their shoulders towered a statue of Anubis, seated upon a throne of skulls, staring before him with jackal eyes, tongue lolling from his jackal mouth.

The priest-women clustered about her, urged her forward. Nita wondered for a wild moment what would happen if she ran along this narrow scarlet gangway and took a running dive into the midst of that mad crowd. Death probably, quickly, at the hands of a dozen madmen. And what awaited her as the bride of Anubis? Death, too. Of that there could be no doubt, and death by some lingering torture.

Then as the madness raced through her blood, she saw she was not to be placed alone upon the knees of the god. Nephtasu already had been fettered to the right leg of the monster with silver chains. The Egyptienne stood looking blankly out over the heads of the mob. Then death was not to come at once! Nita smiled, decided that for a while at least, she would live. Why, she had been a coward; she the Spider's mate, a coward! She must fight on to the bitterest of ends....

Calmly, with the tread of a goddess, she walked the scarlet path and was fastened with chains of silver to the left knee of the seated god. The knee rose as high as her shoulders from the platform, and the chains were fastened by jeweled bracelets to her wrists. She felt the quivering of the platform beneath her feet, was aware of the men who supported this intolerable weight upon their shoulders.

When the scarlet priestesses left, there was a murmur through the crowd—a slow, rising chant. The platform moved forward, crept at a crawling pace through the streets of Mojave and turned laboriously down beside the chuckling water of the little Madres River that presently would gasp out its life in the hot sands....

The procession began to take form. Before the litter of Anubis with its two chained women marched the scarlet priests, before them all was Jackson Grant, with a purple-striped headdress bound with a scarlet fillet. Behind him walked three almost naked men. The central one wore the headdress of a Pharaoh, strode forward with the proud carriage of a king. Nita realized, with a start, that it was Jamid Bey! What, chained, too? Were they all then the prey of this idiot priest, Jackson Grant? But that was impossible. He had bowed and cringed before Nephtasu.

Unwillingly, sternly, Nita turned her head toward the Egyptienne. She was chained, but the link at her wrists was a mere hook which she could detach at will. It was all trumpery then, these chains for Nephtasu and Jamid Bey. Only Nita's chains bound her, irretrievably, to the knees of the cruel god of death and darkness. The hymns rose into the vast dome of brazen sky and was swallowed in its immensity. As far behind as Nita could see, the long black line of human beings followed the litter of Anubis and before them... before them stretched the desert!

Suddenly overwhelmingly, Nita understood and the realization made her reel and sob out an appeal to God above. This bridal procession of Anubis would march out and out into the desert, until the hot sands and the blistering sun overpowered the last mortal man, until they fell fainting prey to the vultures that would gather presently! Jackson Grant and this hellcat chained with false fetters that were no manacles at all; Jamid Bey, would have arranged an escape. But they would massacre Mojave to the last child.

A whole city marched to its death, chanting the damnable hymn to Anubis!

## CHAPTER 18
## ANUBIS' OTHER FACE

A S THE realization burst upon Nita's soul, a madness swept over her. She fought her chains and shrieked at the un-responding heavens. Torture she had been prepared for, still could face. It was not against that which she fought, but against the enormity of a whole city being led out to die by the most cruel torture known to man, the horror of thirst and burning heat beneath the desert sun.

She screamed and her cries were swallowed up in singing.

She lunged about as the half-hundred soldiers that carried the burden of her weight wavered a little and held firm. She yanked at the silver fetters which bound her to this travesty of an idol, and they only bit into her wrists. After a while, the first edge of her terror passed and she strove for more balance, more strength for the battle. Already the fierce straight rays of the sun were eating into her tender flesh, already the dryness of thirst was upon her, sharpened by the shouting.

She leaned back against the knee of Anubis, drew in deep, long breaths to steady herself. Personal hope she had none, chained as she was, but there was no need for these thousands to die. Madness would not help them, but perhaps… She had a glimmering of an idea, and smiling with tight lips, stood away from the statue, began a high, clear intonation of words that had a piercing, a dramatic quality, soaring even above the volume of the chant. She sent her appeal into those deaf ears about her and there was only one basis on which she could plead….

"The bride of Anubis speaks to you," Nita intoned. "She speaks with the tongue of Anubis. Listen and hear what Anubis says through the tongue of his bride…" She saw a few wooden heads swing her way, a few feet already stumbling through the hot sands faltered as they turned. She reiterated her challenge with her clear, carrying voice until even the priests were gazing back at her over their shoulders.

"Listen," she chanted, "ye true believers in the mighty Anubis, hark to the words that the great god speaks through the tongue of his bride. He gives gracious thanks for all the praise which you bestow…."

Nita knew, suddenly, that she had the ears of the multitude about her—knew that they were listening and understanding what she said. It was now that she must strike her blow, now or there was no chance hereafter....

"Anubis speaks to you," she cried. "He bids you look to your priest. He bids you see that this man has refused the sacrifice he would have you make. See, his head is covered and his shoulders refuse the benediction of the sacrifice...!"

Nita flung up her arm to point and the silver bracelets jingled, the chain swung. She pointed with her whole body toward where Grant marched ahead, cowled and gowned against the heat of sun.

"Anubis sayeth: What sort of man is this that he refuses my sacrifice? Is he greater than the bride of Anubis? Than the Queen of Egypt? Than its king? Truly, this man puts himself above Anubis himself!"

Nita caught the quick response of the mob about her. Their faces swung toward the high priest of Anubis and saw his cowl and robes. A great cry went up from them.

Grant turned to face them and the accusing finger of Nita. Without a moment's hesitation, he stripped off cowl and robe and hurled them to the sand. He raised his hands, his great voice booming a command, his whole, gaunt, hard-muscled body enforcing the movement of his arms.

"What Anubis demands, that he shall have," he cried. "In my humility, I did not dare to disrobe, did not dare to offer myself as a sacrifice...."

The crowd was mollified. Grant had foiled her in one

thing, but Nita felt a gleam of hope, the beginning of a vision of escape, of rescue for these poor, mad folk who eddied and danced about the altar of Anubis and his bride. For though Grant had succeeded in turning aside the tide of anger she had raised against him, she had achieved one great advantage. *He had admitted that she was the voice of Anubis!*

Nita felt power thrill over her, but she made no attempt now to cry again above the chanting of the multitude that rose joyfully, ringingly. When they tired, when the fierce heat and the burning of the sun began to afflict them, she would try again, tell them that they had made sacrifice enough, that they had met the tests of their god, Anubis, and that now they might return to their homes. She shrank back into the protective shadow on Anubis, guarding her body against the killing rays of the sun. Life was strong within her. Why, with her voice alone, she might save these thousands!

She was sure suddenly of success and felt a mild surprise that not long ago she had contemplated death. She had only to lift her voice at the proper time....

Through the surge of the chanting, the voice of Nephtasu cut, "If you cry out once more to the people, I'll put a bullet through your pretty cheeks so that you'll never speak again. And don't think anyone will interfere. Grant will tell them Anubis has stricken you for claiming powers you don't possess."

Nita's scornful, confident eyes swung toward Nephtasu and suddenly fear sprang up to keep her company on this slow, burning march to death. Nephtasu leveled an automatic in her right hand.

186

Nita smiled at her with slow, mocking lips, but she made no reply. Not even that would stop her. If only these chains did not bind her wrists! She tested the links and they held firmly. If they would not yield, perhaps the limb of the God to which they were fastened... Nephtasu's cruel green eyes were upon her, the gun ready in her hand. As long as she kept watch, Nita could do nothing, nothing....

Anger at her helplessness swept her—anger that fought with despair for the possession of her soul. Had she battled this far only to fail in the end? The procession crawled on and Nephtasu's keen watch did not relax. Once Nita saw her steal a drink from a bottle hid in a cavity in the leg of Anubis. Her own body cried out for liquid. But she remained motionless, crouched in the shadow of Anubis. Out there, men and women and children toiled through the thick, hot sand and their bared shoulders were exposed to the merciless assault of the sun's rays. Surely, madness could go no further than this, but they still chanted, chanted, chanted....

A heavy drumming of airplane engines raised her hopes for long moments, but when the machine slid by on the edge of the horizon, she recognized it for one of the Egyptienne's ships. So that was how the leaders planned to escape from the death trap they had set for others? Well, Nita would have something to say about that—as the bride of Anubis—if they left her alive at their departure. So she counseled her despair....

The plane vanished into the heat mirage that danced pitilessly all about them and after that the march dragged on interminably. The sun soared until it stood almost over head. The shadow of Anubis which protected Nita shrank back into his belly. The heat struck like a hammer. Still the marchers tramped on, their chant reduced to a hoarse croaking. The continuance of the march became an incredible thing, an impossibility that nevertheless existed. The men who carried the platform dragged their feet, lurching and swaying, but there were too many for the faltering of one to cause disaster. The altar braced them while it bore them down.

NITA TURNED her head heavily toward Nephtasu, standing straight and glorious in the sun. She had had frequent resort to her hidden water supply and she seemed to welcome the lash of the heat. Her eyes were on Nita. The automatic kept unwavering watch. Words stammered up from Nita's dry throat and the sounds came out cracked and unreal.

"For every tortured breath these thousands breathe, you shall breath a thousand in hell," she rasped. "And you'll have no secret water bottle to help you there."

Nephtasu smiled sweetly. "Personally, my dear, I am a realist. I don't believe in hell."

Nita's shoulders sagged. Her legs gave way beneath her at a lurch of the platform and she fell to her knees, braced against the leg of Anubis. The altar was rocking like a ship, as another and yet another of the men who bore it tumbled to the sand to rise no more. But the rest staggered on… Death was very close to all now, its breath the hot, sand-bearing wind of the desert….

Nita moaned in her throat, hopeless eyes staring out at the white sand that was everywhere, sending up pulsations of heat waves to greet the burning sun. This, then, was the end. She felt a stab of regret that she had done no more, knew a moment's bitter anguish for the happiness of life that had been denied her. She swayed, clasping her chained hands....

"Dick," she whispered. "Oh, Dick...!"

She heard vaguely the taunting laughter of Nephtasu, heard Grant begin to boom out the death chant of Anubis again and knew that the end must be near. Soon he and Nephtasu and Jamid Bey would stride away to the plane and leave the rest of them to die miserably. Nita lifted her flinching eyes, gazed upward to the heavens. The sky was dotted by scores of black vultures, circling, circling. Already back there in the wake of the procession, they must have... come down.

Nita shuddered. Her tongue was a thick, strangling thing in her mouth. Heat was doing mad things to her brain.

For instance, there on the horizon, where the dune thrust up against the white line of desert and sky, she could see another Anubis, like the one to which she was chained. Idly she watched, with swooning senses, and Anubis came on, striding, spurning the sand with his great feet, his bronzed body shining in the sunlight, his jackal head....

HIGH, QUIVERING moan pushed its way from Nita's parched lips and she thrust fiercely to her feet, staring, staring. But, good lord, it couldn't be a mirage! A mirage floated in the air and this, this thing... She could see the little spurts of sand as its feet struck. The flash of a sunbeam on Anubis' jeweled belt blinded her. And still the god came on, fully twice the height of a man, great barrel chest bared to the sun. Nita tried to speak and achieved only a dismal croaking. She bit at her tongue and blood opened her throat….

*"Anubis!"* she cried thickly. *"The great Anubis comes!"*

She felt a quivering exultation in every inch of her body. Her clearing eyes told her that the marching figure moved stiffly, that the legs were too short for the towering body. This was no vision… But God, it couldn't be another trick of these masters of chicanery. It *couldn't* be! Victory was already within their grasp.

She whirled toward Nephtasu and saw terror, then shrewdness on her face. The Egyptienne lifted her voice, but it was drowned in the uproar of many thousands of voices shouting the name of Anubis. The platform lurched to the sands as its bearers prostrated themselves, all, all flung down save only Nephtasu, Nita and Grant. Jamid Bey kneeled, but he had been dragged down by the men chained on either hand….

There was terror and exaltation, too, in the thousands about the altar, but it was joy which ruled.

Then, from that stalking great figure, a deep and mighty voice boomed forth. It sent the chant of Anubis resounding over the heads of the multitudes and Nita, hearing, dropped upon her knees and bowed her head in joyful hands.

"Dick, Oh, Dick…!" she cried. For the voice that boomed from the jackal jaws of Anubis was the voice of Richard Wentworth!

Nita was suddenly aware of sharp pistol shots that smashed through the great roar of voices which caught up the chant of Anubis. She twisted her head, saw that Nephtasu, sunk upon one knee, was firing deliberate spaced shots into the belly of the on-striding god. Nita pulled frantically at her chains, surging against the fetters that bound her, and she felt them yield, whirled about to see that the monster's leg had caved in. It was made only of papier-mâché! She struggled even more desperately, but it would yield no more.

Sobs were in her throat as she flung herself down upon her knees and felt feverishly of the leg to see what still held her. She discovered a metal rod brace, over which paper shell had been built. It was bolted to the platform. But what, what about the knee! Perhaps it came apart then. The shots of Nephtasu were exclamation points for her sobs.

Within the hollow shell of the figure, Nita's fingers found the steel frame and followed it upward to the knee joint. It was fastened by a bolt and—thank God—a wing nut! A nut, made to be twisted with the hand alone. It was tight, tight, but she closed her fingers upon it with a frenzy of strength….

Behind her, she heard the booming, magnified voice of Wentworth conclude the chant and begin hurling words at the thousands. Words and maledictions.

"Fools! Have I not enough work to do without fifty thousand souls to judge and send to hell! By Isis and Osiris, it is enough work to kill a god! And this false priest…."

NITA'S BREATH came in frantic gasps while the gun of Nephtasu continued to blast. Obviously, Wentworth was wearing armor. Only let Nephtasu not think to shoot at his mouth! Please, God, don't let her think of that—as Nita already had thought. Oh, this tiny nut, this wretched nut that will not, simply will not turn. Heart-breaking work this, to struggle with a nut that could mean life or death to her and the man she loved; to all these poor suffering humans that Wentworth had come miraculously to save....

*"Traitor to Anubis! Kill me this Jackson Grant! I will joy to send his soul to hell! Offer him up as a sacrifice to Anubis!"*

Nita dropped her numbed fingers from the nut for a long moment, while she shut her lips and fought for calmness. Then she attacked the thing again. Ridiculous that so much should hang on so little. God, ah, God, you couldn't...! Ah! Nita's pant of triumph was enormous in her own ears. The nut was loose! With quick, wrenching hands, she disjointed the knee, threw all her weight into a heave on the papier-mâché shell....

A renewed burst of shooting now; the scream of a dying man and the worshipful shout of thousands. Wentworth's voice crying down the single voice of the multitude.

"It is enough!" he boomed. "Go home. The sacrifice of the priest is enough. In your path, you will find water that I have brought for you. Pure, cold water for your parched tongues and bodies. Go, go as you have come...!"

The sawing of the chain in Nita's hands bit through the hard paper shell. With a final wrench, it tore free and she whirled, panting, the silver chain clutched like a flail. The worshiping people were singing, turning back. It only needed one last word from Wentworth. Nephtasu lifted the automatic, aimed at Anubis' mouth... With a scream like a panther, Nita leaped forward, slashing downward with the silver chain. But Nephtasu stood firm—the bullet sped and the voice of Anubis stopped.

The chain struck the woman's arm, wrapped about it, cut it to the bone.

Deliberately Nita sprang backward, yanking on the chain. Pain forced Nephtasu's lips open. She gasped, took a reeling step forward and went down on her face. The chain came slowly free from her hand and dangled against Nita's legs, a tinkling silver chain smeared with red....

Nita threw up her arms and lifted her voice in a long, singing shout. *"Anubis! Hear thy bride!"*

The great, jackal head of Anubis swung toward her and the long right arm of the god lifted in benediction.

"Your sacrifice has been accepted," she chanted to the mob. "It has been found good in the eyes of Anubis. Turn ye back now to your homes—to the water and the feast that Anubis has prepared for ye. To the water... *water... water...!"*

And amid the crowds that packed about the fallen platform, the voices caught up her refrain: *water from Anubis!* Nita picked out three among the faces before her.

"You are appointed priest of Anubis—and you and you—to take the places of these false men who have misled us. It is the bride of Anubis who speaks. Go, go back and feast on the water of Anubis. Lead them back, oh my priests!"

THERE WAS a joy singing through her now, for Wentworth still stood upon those prodigious bronzed limbs of Anubis. Though the shot had smothered his great voice, he was still there and now he moved heavily forward, his massive hands lifted in a benediction and a threat. Before the marching colossus, the people turned and followed the lead of the few Nita had singled out, began to stream back toward the city, toward the water Wentworth had promised them.

Nephtasu was gone. Jackson Grant fell finally before the assault of the two chained slaves, his throat torn open by their fury.

With faltering steps, Nita stepped from the platform into burning sand that stung her feet. Her sun-weary eyes moved over the scene once more and she saw a woman fleeing toward the sand dune from which Wentworth had come in his strange gear of Anubis. She realized that the woman was Nephtasu, but at that moment the thought meant nothing to her. Only one thing was important, that she should reach Dick…!

Her legs gave way under her and she crawled with hanging head. Something got in her way and she tried wearily to circumvent it, but her last strength had gone into that admonition to the people.

Nita realized that the obstacle in her path was a man's body, the body of Jamid Bey. There was a great, blood-welling wound in his chest, and he was pumping out words to her with his dying breaths….

"Listen, Nita, listen… This is important… This is life and death…" His voice creaked like a rusty hinge, and Nita stopped trying to crawl around his body and with an effort focused eyes and ears on his voice.

"Half the snake is dead—half died with Nephtasu and Grant… but the other part… the head of the snake lives on. It has the money, the drug…" He lay, panting, and Nita said nothing, unable to speak though thoughts milled in her brain like panicked sheep. So it was only half done! All these gargantuan labors, and only half of the job was done. The head of the snake....

"Listen, listen... I lied to Wentworth, with a gun at my back. Acid only intensifies suicide drug. Alkaline... stops it."

A shadow fell across Nita, a shadow that lifted the heat from her burning flesh like a cool blanket. She raised her head to peer into the jackal face of Anubis....

"Dick, Dick," she cried despairingly. "He says the head of the snake,—the head of the snake still lives! And Nephtasu is running toward the plane. I saw her. Dear God, Dick, don't let us fail now...!"

A whisper in the sand and Ram Singh ran up, shouting.

"Another plane!" he rasped. "Another plane has landed, *sahib.*"

"I was expecting it," Wentworth's voice was deep and hollow within the mask, but not loud since the bullet had smashed the radio magnifier. "Ram Singh, I give the *missie sahib* into your care. Guard her well."

Nita sagged against Ram Singh and he caught her up in his arms. She felt the swift, long strides of his running as he sped back toward the dune, toward the ship. She turned her tired head, stared at the retreating figure of Anubis that seemed to stumble in the sand as it ran. She was aware that the right arm of Anubis had fallen to the ground and that in its place was a hand with a gun, Dick's hand....

THE SECOND plane was a hundred yards away from the one that Wentworth had halted just behind the dune, Nephtasu was half the distance toward the second ship, and beside Wentworth's craft, stood a gigantic figure of a man, tall but seeming almost short with the sagging weight of great scallops and balloons of fat that swelled within his tight clothing. Each arm was like a great, swollen thigh and the rifle that he held in his hands was a little stick....

Nita saw these things as she crested the dune, borne by the faithful Ram Singh. Even above the panting of the Hindu, she heard the deep voice of Wentworth and the high, querulous tremolo of Craft Elliott. It was Wentworth who was speaking.

"You have preyed upon humanity too long, Elliott," he said heavily. "It was not Nephtasu, but I who sent you the telegram bidding you come."

"Fool!" Elliott piped up at him, sweat streaking his huge face. "Fool! Didn't come... for her. Came... to help you...."

The figure of Anubis seemed to lean forward a little. "Listen, Elliott, I sent a telegram from Delron City and told you simply 'Come. Treachery!' and signed it 'Nephtasu.'"

*"If you are not guilty, how did you know where to come?"*

"Another thing, Elliott," Wentworth's hollow voice boomed. "When I rescued Denver Dane, I was fired on by an incredibly good rifleman. Sneed Jenkins tells me that you are more than expert...."

Elliott gasped: "Sneed... Jenkins!" The rifle was almost in line now. In another split second, it would blast death up into the body of the Spider. Nita threw herself from Ram Singh's arms, cupped her hands to her mouth, shouted down the dune's slope.

"Danger, Elliott... Behind you...!"

It was a bluff. Nita's hand pointed off toward the second plane

196

and now for the first time since her glance on topping the dune, she turned that way. Sneed Jenkins and Nephtasu were running across the sand and even as Nita shouted, Jenkins popped into the side doorway and a moment later the mounting roar of the engine reached their ears. Dust swept in a whirlwind back from the plane's propellers, almost sweeping Nephtasu from her feet. But it was obvious that Jenkins waited for her. Elliott swung about with movements incredibly quick and light for his bulk and the rifle came to his shoulder. Nita saw the thrust of its recoil and, with its sharp crack, saw a glass burst in the cockpit of the plane. Jenkins disappeared; the propellers ceased their whirlwind fire. Nephtasu whirled about, staring back across the sands. Elliott had ended that treachery....

The hugely fat man executed his lightning again, rifle thrusting upward, a toy in his great hands. Twice the Spider's automatic blasted from the arm socket of Anubis. The rifle fell from Elliott's arms and spots of blood marked his shoulders. Ram Singh sped down the hillside and Nita raced beside him, flanking the great hulking figure of Anubis.

"Tell me one thing, Elliott," Wentworth's cold voice commanded. "The whereabouts of the suicide drug. Tell me that and you shall live."

Elliott looked up at him with the fat mouth drawn into a pained, wrathful purse. He appeared insulted.

"Live?... Live?" he gasped out a laugh that shook the mountain of his body. "Live? What do I... care about living...? You have broken my arms... With them, my art dies... My fat... never set them right...."

He turned away from Wentworth, reeled drunkenly across the sands….

"Elliott," Wentworth shouted. "Turn back or I'll kill you."

"Kill… and be damned…!" Elliott's thin voice floated back. "I don't know the drug…! Jenkins… Jenkins and that woman!"

**HE WHEEZED** his way heavily along, pushing, heaving at his heavy feet, sweat streaming down with his blood. Nephtasu stayed where she had stopped at the murder of Jenkins, waiting as coolly as death. Her arm that Nita had chain lashed was tucked behind her, her head was high. The four labored across the sands toward her. The towering figure of Anubis and the fat man, Nita and Ram Singh… After a while, Nephtasu started toward them, running a little, her face toward Elliott, one hand stretched toward him.

"Elliott," she cried, "they have shot you…! Elliott, my love…!"

Nita felt sickness strike at the pit of her stomach. *Elliott, my love!* She slowed in her walking, for Nephtasu had reached Elliott and now was reaching upward for his neck with one arm. Then suddenly, Nephtasu whirled, throwing up an automatic. She was shielded behind the body of Elliott and she aimed at Nita's heart.

"Fool!" she cried. "Do you think you can destroy me and live? Do you…?"

Elliott toppled forward and Nephtasu screamed and fought frantically to escape. Her gun belched with a muffled sound; then Elliott fell on top of her. Her cry was mashed into nothingness. No part of her was visible. The man's great, swollen body had overwhelmed her, buried her. He lay there, panting.

The shell fell from the figure of Anubis and a great black Negro, face shining with sweat, lifted Wentworth down from a light chair that was fitted and strapped to his shoulders. He set Wentworth upon his feet and Nita ran to his side, stood staring in horror down at the quivering mound of flesh that was Elliott.

Ram Singh was tugging futilely at Elliott's shoulders, trying to turn him. Now George rushed to the task, but the fat only squeezed out from under their hands. They could do nothing.

"Might as well let me alone," Elliott gasped. "I'm dying... she shot... shot me... treachery... can stand... but mockery... Did you hear her?" Elliott twisted about his fat head and the effort exhausted him so that he lay panting for long seconds. Ram Singh and George were upon their knees now, scooping out handfuls of sand so that Elliott could roll to one side. "Mocked me... called me her love... and she made fun of me once... me and my fat...."

Wentworth stood helplessly by while the men labored. But they all knew it was hopeless. Nephtasu had been crushed by the man she and Jenkins had misled, smothered by his fatness. Nita shuddered and turned her back, her mind flew back to the thousands trekking across the desert.

"You promised them water, Dick... Oh, Dick, I had no hope that you'd come."

Wentworth nodded. "My plane cracked up six hundred miles from Mojave, but I hit a hay barn and nothing serious happened except to the plane. I got another and rushed on to Mojave and found the whole city had strolled out into the desert. I stopped the tail end of the procession with my figure of Anubis, got word through to the state capital and troops are bringing water out into the desert. As soon as that was arranged I flew on ahead...."

"But the telegram to Elliott. What made you suspect him?"

Wentworth shook his head somberly. "I didn't suspect him any more than several others, but I sent them all telegrams, saying simply 'Come. Treachery.' Apparently Elliott was the only one who knew where to come. And there was treachery—Sneed Jenkins and Nephtasu were the powers behind Anubis."

Ram Singh came toward them. "Wah! He died like a soldier, that fat one," he said. "The woman is... dead."

Nita was still shuddering at the horror of Nephtasu's death. She urged Dick toward their plane. "I still don't understand why all this was done. It's... it's fiendish."

"Money!" Wentworth said succinctly. It seems that some one—Craft Elliott and Jenkins, we know now—hid a gigantic scheme to dominate all industry. The wholesale deaths were both a screen and a means of accomplishing their ends. It's incredible that men should grow so rabid for money.

"But remember that Nephtasu comes of an ancient, cruel race. She actually was a daughter of the Pharaohs, and Elliott's sensitiveness about fat had turned him into a monster who hungered for power, power, power to prove that his bodily distortion was unimportant... I doubt that any of this would have happened, however, if Sneed Jenkins had not been ambitious...."

**THEY HAD** reached the plane now and Wentworth laboriously climbed inside, found a wrap for Nita. Ram Singh preceded George, went straight to the cockpit while the Negro toiled laboriously into a seat. He sat there panting, fanning himself with his hand, grinning widely. All the deaths seemed to have made no impression upon him.

"Ma'am?" he answered Nita's question as to why he smiled. "Well, they's two reasons, and both of'em good. Mr. Wentworth done promised me a fortune and I knows he's good for it. That's one almighty good reason, and the other"—his grin widened, his white teeth showing—"Ma'am them Harlem boys goin' to fall dead with envy when I tells 'em about playing god!"

## POPULAR HERO PULPS  AVAILABLE NOW:

### THE SPIDER

| | |
|---|---|
| ❏ #1: The Spider Strikes | $13.95 |
| ❏ #2: The Wheel of Death | $13.95 |
| ❏ #3: Wings of the Black Death | $13.95 |
| ❏ #4: City of Flaming Shadows | $13.95 |
| ❏ #5: Empire of Doom! | $13.95 |
| ❏ #6: Citadel of Hell | $13.95 |
| ❏ #7: The Serpent of Destruction | $13.95 |
| ❏ #8: The Mad Horde | $13.95 |
| ❏ #9: Satan's Death Blast | $13.95 |
| ❏ #10: The Corpse Cargo | $13.95 |
| ❏ #11: Prince of the Red Looters | $13.95 |
| ❏ #12: Reign of the Silver Terror | $13.95 |
| ❏ #13: Builders of the Dark Empire | $13.95 |
| ❏ #14: Death's Crimson Juggernaut | $13.95 |
| ❏ #15: The Red Death Rain | $13.95 |
| ❏ #16: The City Destroyer | $13.95 |
| ❏ #17: The Pain Emperor | $13.95 |
| ❏ #18: The Flame Master | $13.95 |
| ❏ #19: Slaves of the Crime Master | $13.95 |
| ❏ #20: Reign of the Death Fiddler | $13.95 |
| ❏ #21: Hordes of the Red Butcher | $13.95 |
| ❏ #22: Dragon Lord of the Underworld | $13.95 |
| ❏ *NEW:* #23: Master of the Death-Madness | $13.95 |

### THE MYSTERIOUS WU FANG

| | |
|---|---|
| ❏ #1: The Case of the Six Coffins | $12.95 |
| ❏ #2: The Case of the Scarlet Feather | $12.95 |
| ❏ #3: The Case of the Yellow Mask | $12.95 |
| ❏ #4: The Case of the Suicide Tomb | $12.95 |
| ❏ #5: The Case of the Green Death | $12.95 |
| ❏ #6: The Case of the Black Lotus | $12.95 |
| ❏ #7: The Case of the Hidden Scourge | $12.95 |

### G-8 AND HIS BATTLE ACES

| | |
|---|---|
| ❏ #1: The Bat Staffel | $13.95 |

### CAPTAIN SATAN

| | |
|---|---|
| ❏ #1: The Mask of the Damned | $13.95 |
| ❏ #2: Parole for the Dead | $13.95 |
| ❏ #3: The Dead Man Express | $13.95 |
| ❏ #4: A Ghost Rides the Dawn | $13.95 |
| ❏ #5: The Ambassador From Hell | $13.95 |

### CAPTAIN ZERO

| | |
|---|---|
| ❏ #1: City of Deadly Sleep | $13.95 |
| ❏ #2: The Mark of Zero! | $13.95 |

### OPERATOR 5

| | |
|---|---|
| ❏ #1: The Masked Invasion | $13.95 |
| ❏ #2: The Invisible Empire | $13.95 |
| ❏ #3: The Yellow Scourge | $13.95 |
| ❏ #4: The Melting Death | $13.95 |
| ❏ #5: Cavern of the Damned | $13.95 |
| ❏ #6: Master of Broken Men | $13.95 |
| ❏ #7: Invasion of the Dark Legions | $13.95 |
| ❏ #8: The Green Death Mists | $13.95 |
| ❏ #9: Legions of Starvation | $13.95 |
| ❏ #10: The Red Invader | $13.95 |
| ❏ #11: The League of War-Monsters | $13.95 |
| ❏ *NEW:* #12: The Army of the Dead | $13.95 |

### DUSTY AYRES AND HIS BATTLE BIRDS

| | |
|---|---|
| ❏ #1: Black Lightning! | $13.95 |
| ❏ #2: Crimson Doom | $13.95 |
| ❏ #3: The Purple Tornado | $13.95 |
| ❏ #4: The Screaming Eye | $13.95 |
| ❏ #5: The Green Thunderbolt | $13.95 |
| ❏ #6: The Red Destroyer | $13.95 |
| ❏ #7: The White Death | $13.95 |
| ❏ #8: The Black Avenger | $13.95 |
| ❏ #9: The Silver Typhoon | $13.95 |
| ❏ #10: The Troposphere F-S | $13.95 |
| ❏ #11: The Blue Cyclone | $13.95 |
| ❏ #12: The Tesla Raiders | $13.95 |

### DR. YEN SIN

| | |
|---|---|
| ❏ #1: Mystery of the Dragon's Shadow | $12.95 |
| ❏ #2: Mystery of the Golden Skull | $12.95 |
| ❏ #3: Mystery of the Singing Mummies | $12.95 |

### MAVERICKS

| | |
|---|---|
| ❏ #1: Five Against the Law | $12.95 |
| ❏ #2: Mesquite Manhunters | $12.95 |
| ❏ #3: Bait for the Lobo Pack | $12.95 |
| ❏ #4: Doc Grimson's Outlaw Posse | $12.95 |
| ❏ #5: Charlie Parr's Gunsmoke Cure | $12.95 |